NOTHING VENTURED

(or the liberation of a very boring man)

ELISABETH C. THOMPSON

ATLANTIS PUBLICATIONS

Nothing Ventured

ISBN : 978-0-9556971-0-4

Published by:
Atlantis Publications
11, Guildford Place
Chichester
West Sussex
PO19 5DU

A CIP catalogue record of this book
can be obtained from the British Library.

Designed & produced by Michael Walsh at
THE BETTER BOOK COMPANY

a division of
RPM Print & Design
2-3 Spur Road
Chichester
West Sussex
PO19 8PR

For Jonathan, Andrew, Jenni, Laura and Ashley, but most of all for my long suffering husband, Jeffrey, without whom none of this would have been possible.

1

Something made him look up. It was a ray of sunlight glinting off the cream and orange jug on the dresser, one of his mother's favourites. He remembered the day she had bought it many years ago, when they had been on holiday in Devon and a reluctant smile warmed the icy reaches of his saddened eyes. He and his brother had earned a bag of sweets each that day for waiting quietly while she had searched the dingy little shop for treasures.

After the death of his widowed mother, Ian Chisholm was contemplating the future; something he did, it seemed, with monotonous regularity lately. His brother was always telling him to get a life, but how was he to do it? Mike was already set up. He had a wife, two lovely children and his own building company, it was easy for him to talk.

Ian's parents had been careful with their money and his mother had left him their house and a nice little nest egg to share with his brother. That, combined with his recently received redundancy payment would mean that he did not have to look for another job immediately and money was not a problem, so for the first time in his life he had the welcome opportunity to choose how he would like to spend his time, if only he could work out what that was.

The jug though, had given him an idea and he finally got his brain in gear and made a decision. He would declutter the house and claim it for his own. It was full of old furniture that was not to his taste and endless bits of china his mother, an inveterate charity shop browser, had picked up for next to nothing over the years and proudly displayed on her carefully polished shelves; but up until now Ian had not felt brave enough to tackle any sort of change.

Well, today was the day, he thought positively as he brushed the toast crumbs from his fingers, tidied up the breakfast dishes and headed for the attic. He was sure there would be a box up there he could use to pack up the ornaments, and then he would check the phone book for the number of his nearest auction house. Perhaps he could get someone out to look over the furniture too – he had watched this scenario unfold recently on daytime television. His brother, who had never understood his mother's fascination for 'old tat' as he called it, had given Ian a free rein with the sorting out when he finally got round to it, so in fact it was all down to him, now he was ready to do it . After all, as his mother had always been so fond of telling him, 'nothing ventured, nothing gained'.

Having made a plan at last after weeks of wavering, Ian felt full of enthusiasm to carry it out and he made his way upstairs, retrieved the loft ladder from its hiding place, and then climbed through the loft hatch to have a good look around. It was quite gloomy up there under the eaves and it took a while for his eyes to become accustomed to the meagre amount of light given out by the 40-watt bulb, now festooned with cobwebs, that his father had rigged up as a temporary measure many years before.

He looked past the folded up carpet, boxes of Christmas decorations, rolls of old wallpaper, his sets of well used Meccano, piles of children's books, some broken toys, a couple of suitcases and the rocking horse he and Mike had once shared, his eyes finally settling on a large box that had been put up in the attic by his father 'just in case'. It had once contained their television set and Ian reckoned it was the ideal size for transporting the bits and pieces he had in mind for the auction house. It was full of polystyrene packing, which Ian tugged out unceremoniously and left on the dusty floor behind him as he manoeuvred his way precariously down the rickety loft ladder with his prize.

When he was safely on the landing Ian turned off the light and sent the ladder up again, shutting the loft hatch with a bang. Now all he needed was a pile of old newspapers to wrap up his mother's treasures. Thank goodness, he thought to himself, for the recycling bin and the much maligned fortnightly collection.

He wrapped each item with care, and it wasn't long before the shelves were empty and the box was full. Ian felt a pang of regret mixed with a certain excitement at moving on, something he now realised had been long overdue. Next, he thumbed through the phone book and discovered there was an auction house quite near to his local market. It was called McFarlane & Sons and reassuringly declared 'Monthly Sales of Selected Antiques, Fine Art and Collectables'. He dialled the number and waited.

"McFarlanes", said the voice on the other end of the telephone. It sounded young, efficient and definitely female. "Can I help you?"

"I hope so," said Ian hesitantly, "I have a few bits of china I would like you to sell in your next auction, but I am not quite sure how I go about it."

"Just bring them in to the office," said the voice crisply. "One of our auctioneers will have a look at them for you and we can take it from there."

Ian gave her his name and home telephone number and arranged to take his box full of china into their offices that morning for a valuation and possible inclusion in their next auction, which would be held in ten days' time. He put the phone down, pleased with himself and relieved that it had all been much easier than he had imagined and much less intimidating.

Linchester was a medium-sized town with many attractive features, including its own cathedral, theatre, market and some Roman remains. Wednesday was market day and the town was full of shoppers so he had difficulty parking the car, but just as he was about to give up hope of finding a space in which to park, he saw a car indicating and pulling out right outside the auction house. He grabbed the place quickly, unloaded his box, locked the car and headed for the open doors of McFarlane & Sons.

The auction hall was deserted apart from some old upholstered chairs, a couple of chandeliers, a large mahogany dining table, some watercolours hanging from the walls and a row of Toby Jugs staring down at him from a high shelf. Ian could hear muffled voices coming from the front of the hall, and made his way awkwardly into a small office with his box.

"I phoned earlier," he said hopefully, to no-one in particular leaning his box on a convenient desk. The dark-haired girl sitting at the computer smiled at him and said, "You must be Mr Chisholm. Mr McFarlane, this gentleman has some china to show you."

An elderly man with the distracted air of a university professor who had been looking through some papers at the back of the office, turned round, his eyes homing in on Ian's box.

"Ah, that looks interesting. Bring it through into the hall and I'll have a look at what you've brought with you."

Ian carried his box back into the hall and placed it on the mahogany table. Slowly and carefully James McFarlane unwrapped the various pieces in the box and when they were displayed on the table he asked Ian how much he wanted for them.

"I don't know what they are worth," he said diffidently, "they were my mother's treasures."

"Well, probably sold as one lot, we might get eighty pounds," said the auctioneer hopefully, "... except for this one," and he held up the cream and orange jug that had started Ian on his quest, in order to examine it better in the light. "This one is rather special and in very good condition. I wouldn't be surprised if we get over five thousand pounds for it."

There was a stunned silence from Ian. Five thousand pounds for his mother's jug?

"It is a Clarice Cliff Lotus jug," James went on, "with the 'Sliced Circle' pattern. Look, it is fully marked with the Bizarre stamp and a signature," he said turning it upside down and showing Ian the base. "These are much sought after now you know. We will put it in the auction with a reserve of four thousand five hundred. Is that all right with you?" The colour drained from Ian's face and he replied hesitantly, "Er, yes. Yes thank you, I never expected any of it to be worth that much. I am very happy with that."

They finished the paperwork and Ian left McFarlanes with his receipt and a great deal on his mind. Mike would be amazed. He had been so dismissive of his mother's hobby and Ian could not wait to ring his brother with the news.

When he arrived home he realised that, in all the excitement he had forgotten to ask for an expert to visit the house and inspect the old furniture he wanted to sell. He was determined to make a clean sweep, so he made one last call to McFarlanes and arranged for someone to visit the house the next day. Now for Mike – this was a conversation to which he was really looking forward.

Mike's voice sounded very surprised.

"What? Five thousand pounds?" he yelled down the phone. Ian held it away from his ear.

"Five thousand for that gaudy thing? Surely not. When is the auction being held? This I must see."

"I was surprised myself to tell you the truth but Mr McFarlane the auctioneer, was quite definite about its value. The sale will be Friday week. Anyway, I will see you for lunch on Sunday, won't I? We can talk some more then."

Ian had taken a long time to get over his mother's death and in an effort to cheer him up, Mike and his wife Gaynor, had been inviting Ian round to their house for lunch on Sundays from time to time over the last few months and now it had become a weekly ritual which suited them all.

"Of course. I'm glad you have finally made a start on the house Ian, it's about time. Whatever will you unearth next? Some priceless gem I shouldn't wonder."

"Who knows?" laughed Ian. He was still surprised at how motivated he felt now that he had started the ball rolling. He could not wait to see what would happen the next day; at last his depression seemed to be lifting and optimism was waiting in line, but what the two brothers did not know was that Mike's jocular comments held more than a grain of truth in them.

2

At precisely ten o'clock the following morning, as arranged, the doorbell rang. When Ian opened the door, the first thing he noticed was a mane of red hair, and then a very smart pair of black suede boots containing a shapely pair of long legs.

"Pippa Flynn from McFarlanes. Are you Mr Chisholm?" Ian shook the hand proffered and nodded silently. He ushered his visitor into the front room. His mind was in turmoil. Surely he recognised that name; that face; that glorious auburn hair? It must have been at least thirty years, but he was sure it was the same Philippa Flynn who had been a pupil at North Street Primary all those years ago. She was about three years younger than him, but he had always noticed her in assemblies and in the school choir.

"What was it you wanted us to look at?"

Her voice brought Ian back to the present and he started to talk about the different items he wanted her to examine. There were several chairs, two small tables, one bookcase and upstairs, an old mahogany bedroom suite. Pippa took notes, made sketches, noted measurements and finally took photos with her digital camera. In fact she did her job very thoroughly, he thought.

"I'm sure we will be able to sell all these for you Mr Chisholm, but I can't guarantee how much we will get for them. Large pieces are hard to shift these days. The bookcase should go well though, and the occasional tables. Altogether I would estimate about seven hundred pounds."

Ian thought that was a fair price, if not a bit ambitious for some odd pieces of old furniture and he agreed to go ahead straight away. Pippa quickly made a phone call to check when the furniture could be collected, "Monday OK with you?"

"That should be all right. I have nothing planned for Monday." He sounded like an automaton, he thought, but he seemed incapable of thinking or acting rationally at the moment. He had fallen under her spell.

"Fine, I will give you my card in case there is any problem with the arrangements," she said in a very efficient fashion, handing him a small grey business card with 'McFarlane & Sons, Auctioneers' printed on one side in bold script and her name and telephone number printed on the other. He took the card from her outstretched hand and wondered whether to reveal that he had recognised her. Before he knew what was happening, he heard himself say, "Do you remember Miss Scott?"

"Miss Scott?" she asked quizzically.

"Miss Scott from North Street Primary," he explained.

"My favourite teacher! How do you know her?" asked Pippa startled.

Ian, now out of robot-mode, explained how he had recognised Pippa and offered her a cup of coffee while they chatted.

"Sorry, but I have another appointment in ten minutes," she apologised. "I could meet you later though."

Ian couldn't believe his ears. Another surprise for Mike – his boring little brother being asked out by a gorgeous redhead?

"Tonight at The Ship? I could be there at about six thirty," she went on.

How should he reply? After a small hesitation, he said, "Why not? I'll look forward to it," and as he let her out of the front door, he couldn't quite believe what had happened. Not only was he sorting the house out, it seemed that he was starting to sort out his personal life too. He could not remember the last time, if ever, he had shared an evening out with such an attractive woman and he spent the rest of the day wondering if she would actually turn up and if she did, what they would find to talk about.

The Ship was an old coaching inn at the centre of town, close to the theatre. It had several bars and a good restaurant and Ian had been there many times before, but this time it felt new and exciting. He made sure he was there early and settled himself in a corner by the fire with a good view of the door and sipped absent-mindedly at his beer.

Summer Lightning was a particular favourite of his and he had plenty of time to savour it and watch all the bubbles rise to the top of the glass in the cool clear golden ale as he swallowed the first exquisite mouthful, while he waited for Pippa to arrive. It would be easy for him to notice her coming in as there were only three other people in the bar with him. He thought this was probably because it was too early for the pre-theatre rush, but judging from the delicious aroma of cooking food and coffee percolating at the bar, the evening punters were imminently expected.

Just after half past six the door opened and she was there. Ian stood up as she came over.

"What can I get you?" he asked her with a welcoming smile.

"Just a coffee please, I'm driving," she said, and with that, Pippa took off her coat and sat down. It was the same coat that she had been wearing earlier, so Ian reckoned she must have come straight from work. He went to the bar, ordered the coffee and asked the barman to bring it over to their table, then he rejoined Pippa and asked her amicably, if she'd had a busy day.

"Hectic! I must have driven over a hundred miles. I've seen some really good stuff though, so I think it was worth it. It should be a good auction this month."

Ian told her all about his mother's jug, and she listened attentively. The coffee arrived and they carried on chatting. The conversation ranged from school to music, then work and back to classmates, in fact, they found it hard to stop talking. His earlier worries had obviously been completely unfounded.

Eventually Pippa looked at her watch. "Is it really eight o'clock already? I'm starving; I've had nothing to eat since lunchtime."

"Why don't we have a meal here?" he suggested helpfully, "I am quite hungry myself and I know they do a good varied menu."

"Good idea, I am right behind you."

They strolled over to the restaurant and found themselves a secluded table for two. Over dinner the conversation carried on, this time more along the lines of food, cooking, local pubs and where not to eat.

Eleven o'clock came and went.

Ian didn't want the evening to end at all, but at last he realised time was running out and if he didn't have the courage to ask her out on a proper date, he risked losing the seed of their relationship before it had even germinated. Pippa looked at her watch again and sighed,

"It is getting late and I really must get home. I have an early appointment tomorrow morning and I have to call at the office first to pick up some papers. That was a fabulous meal, Ian, thank you."

Now was his last chance. But no, he couldn't find the words. They parted outside in the road.

"Well, goodbye, and thanks for a lovely evening," Pippa called as she walked over to her car. Then she was gone.

Ian was mad with himself. He really liked her and felt they had got on so well. As he trudged home in the cold gusty wind, he was despondent. His brother was right after all; he really was a very boring man. Why couldn't he be more like Mike? Mike would never have let her leave without first arranging another date. Was she destined to slip out of his life so soon? The thought of never seeing her again was too painful to bear. Ian racked his brains for a solution.

Then it occurred to him. His pace quickened. He felt in his jacket – yes, it was still there! The card Pippa had given him earlier in case of problems was in his pocket. He could ring her in the morning and perhaps by then he would have worked out a strategy.

All was not lost and for the second time in twenty-four hours his mother's favourite maxim was ringing in his ears; he immediately started to walk even faster and on arriving home, let himself in through the front door and closed it firmly behind him with a satisfying thud.

3

Ian did not sleep well. He had put Pippa's card right beside the phone so he could not lose it, but the conundrum of how to ask her out and where they should go, remained unsolved.

Although he did not know it, Pippa was about to solve the problem for him. She was surprised at how much she had enjoyed their evening together and had made up her mind to see him again. Her brother, Tim, had been begging her to go and listen to his band Nimbus for ages and had reminded her only the day before that they were playing at the Drunken Duck on Saturday evening. She thought she would give Ian a ring and see if he fancied going with her, she just had time before her next meeting, but before she could dial his number her phone rang.

"Hi Pippa, where have you been hiding?" asked a friendly female voice.

"Alice, it's good to hear you," replied Pippa warmly, "I haven't been hiding anywhere, but work has been manic lately. Are you psychic? I was going to ring you later. I have news, hot off the press actually and I have been meaning to ring you for ages, but I wouldn't have had much to tell you before." Pippa knew she would not be able to resist telling her best friend what had been going on with Ian. They did not often meet, as Alice was an air hostess, married to a pilot and between the three of them, it was rare for their spare time to coincide. Sometimes months would go by without Pippa and Alice actually making contact.

"I've met this really nice guy and I'm planning to take him with me to hear Tim's band on Saturday," she went on.

"That's wonderful, Pippa. It is a long time since you were even remotely interested in anyone; just give me some background info., where did you meet him? How old is he? Is he local?"

Pippa willingly painted the picture, then Alice explained, "Simon will be back off long haul next week and we could all go out together," but Pippa declined that invitation.

"Not such a good idea. It is early days yet and I think we will keep it low-key for a while."

"Well, I think you should go for it, he sounds perfect. Let me know when Tim is playing next, I'd like to hear him again," and after chatting animatedly for about half an hour, Alice rang off. Pippa, checking the time, realised it would now be another hour before she would be free to ring Ian. Never mind, she thought, Ian would keep, and with that happy thought in her mind, Pippa went into her next meeting.

Ian, meanwhile, was wandering round the house trying to decide what it would look like without the furniture and mulling over possible redecoration plans hoping an idea for a date would come to him, when the phone rang.

As he picked it up he was delighted to recognise Pippa's voice on the other end. She explained about Tim's band and he jumped at the chance to join her on Saturday night. He readily agreed to give her a lift to the Drunken Duck and after she had given him the directions to her flat which was in a new and rather smart development quite near the station, he put the phone down thinking to himself that finally, at the age of thirty-nine, his life was taking on an impetus of its own and he was a very willing victim. He made a mental note not to tell Mike about Pippa yet. He wanted to keep their friendship to himself for a bit – she was too precious to share.

Nevertheless, it was a long time until Saturday night and the mundane tasks of life had to be tackled. Ian needed some supplies, so he drove to the supermarket humming happily to himself and loaded up his trolley with bread, milk, apples, bananas, some salad, a couple of pizzas and half a dozen bottles of beer, then, as an afterthought, he picked up some magazines on house makeovers. They promised him 'Ten Golden Rules for Beginners', and 'Amazing Room Makeovers' which seemed just about right for him, he needed all the inspiration he could get. Now he had started to reinvent himself, he could not stop.

On the journey home everything seemed to be in much sharper focus. Children walking with their parents were smiling happily; babies were chuckling in their prams. The dogs he passed were wagging their tails enthusiastically and every traffic light he approached changed to green.

Back home he cooked himself some pasta and when the saucepans were tidied away he settled down with the magazines. It seemed he could choose between 'making his rooms come alive' and 'transforming his hallway into a light and welcoming space', but in the end he was just confused. He knew Mike employed some painters who could do the work for him but first, it would seem, he had to decide on themes, colours, fabrics and so on.

His parents had always made the decisions on decorating and this usually amounted to a coat of very ordinary cream paint on the walls every two years and white gloss on the woodwork in between. Even the front door had been the same ghastly green for as long as he could remember. Well, Ian was going to change all that but first he had to do his homework.

Where on earth was Anna Ryder Richardson when you needed her? Although it occurred to him on second thoughts, that he was sure Pippa would make an excellent substitute.

Saturday arrived, and with it yet more stormy weather. Ian sighed as he looked out of the kitchen window. February's weather just could not make up its mind. One minute it was pouring with rain and unpleasantly cold, then it was the turn of the wind, followed by even more rain. The interludes heralding the coming of spring were all too brief. Whether the elements were benevolent or malicious, it crossed his mind that on the record so far, it should not be 'global warming' that was the danger, but 'global storming'.

The wind punched at his windows and played the draught excluder his father had tacked around the front door like some unearthly harmonica. To take his mind off it all Ian started thinking about his evening out with Pippa. They had discovered a mutual liking for The Beatles and Coldplay. A particular favourite of hers was Crowded House, but Ian could not claim a favourite as such, he loved music full stop and as a teenager had saved up frantically in order to attend as many pop concerts as possible with his friend, Garth.

Recently there had been times when he had spent days listening to nothing but Bach or Mahler, but now he was ready for a lighter influence and Pippa had explained that Nimbus played cover versions as well as some of their own music, so he was really looking forward to hearing them.

Bother, he realised with a sinking heart, after all the auction excitement his washing had been neglected. Did he have a clean shirt to wear? What about his smart trousers?

Ian hurried up the stairs to check his wardrobe. The Ted Baker shirt he had in mind to wear was, as he had feared, in the washing basket. Fortunately the trousers were fine, so he set about washing his shirt and while he was waiting for it to be dry enough to iron, he started to empty the bookcase which was to go to auction the following week. He had not realised the extent of their so called library and it took him quite a while.

As he was sorting through the books, memories of his parents came flooding back. His father had collected, amongst other things, a complete set of Charles Dickens and some rather nice leather bound volumes of poetry. There were several other very old copies of books that he had been given as a child, *Moby Dick* and *Treasure Island* to name but a few. His mother's taste was represented by some Victorian novelettes, one or two Jane Austens and a few modern family sagas, whereas Ian's contribution consisted of the *Lord of the Rings* Trilogy and several John Le Carre thrillers, although these were just the tip of the iceberg as far as his reading went and over the past few weeks he had got through goodness knows how many different sorts of books. Reading had been his only solace when he had not wanted to venture forth into the outside world.

He had not quite decided what to do with the books. Perhaps they could be included in some future auction? It had also occurred to him that his nieces might like some of them and he decided he would ask Pippa what she thought about it. He found one he had given to his father on his last birthday which was a book of interesting quotes from famous people and one in particular caught his eye, as he read on it struck a chord with him. The quote was from Samuel Johnson, and he had noted, 'A man who has not been in Italy is always conscious of an inferiority, from his not having seen what it is expected a man should see.'

Ian had never been to Italy and he wondered idly if Pippa had; perhaps they could go there together? Lazy days spent on the shores of the Italian Lakes, the sun warming their backs won hands down against a rainy afternoon in Linchester; but first things first, he thought reluctantly, a dose of reality bringing his wishful thinking to an end, Italy could wait but the piles of books would not organise themselves and he carried on with renewed enthusiasm, forming neat piles of books tidily in the hall.

4

Pippa really liked Ian. She had been with her last boyfriend for three years, until she discovered he was cheating on her with two other girls, which had completely knocked her confidence for a while. Most of the other blokes she had been out with were only interested in one thing.

The young auctioneers she came across at work were arrogant and full of their own importance. In fact one of them had called her an 'old-fashioned girl' because she refused to have sex with him.

Ian seemed different and she felt he had hidden depths. He was shy and a bit quiet, but had a good sense of humour; he was kind and caring, but more than that he was intelligent, quirky and they shared the same taste in music and they had a few mutual acquaintances. She couldn't understand how they had never met before.

All in all, she felt very lucky indeed that Ian had popped into her life at this juncture – and all due to a few pieces of brown furniture. Alice had advised her to 'go for it' and that was exactly what she intended to do.

The doorbell rang and Pippa quickly checked her hair in the mirror before she went to open the door.

As it opened, Ian was taken aback for a moment by how lovely Pippa was. Standing there with the light shining on her hair, she looked stunning and he had to mentally pinch himself to see if this was real, or just one of his unfulfilled dreams.

"I'm ready, Ian, I've just got to fetch my coat," said the vision, "Come in and wait for a minute, the fire is on in the lounge," and she ushered him into her tastefully decorated sitting room, then disappeared.

"No hurry," he called after her, pulling himself together. "We've got plenty of time," and he sat down to look around the room. His gaze was attracted to a small antique table with spindly carved legs that stood next to the light beech fire surround. Displayed on the top of the table, in carefully arranged disarray, were various polished silver frames out of which faces, young and old, smiled pleasantly at him. He presumed they were members of Pippa's family, one in particular of a young woman wearing pearls just had to be her mother as she had the same luxuriant auburn hair. He was sure he had seen a silver frame at home somewhere; he would have to see if he could find it. He took in the pale blue paint on the walls, and the modern art she had chosen. The whole effect was stylish and elegant – much like Pippa herself.

It wasn't long before she reappeared wearing a nice warm black wool coat. She knotted a scarf round her neck and Ian moved towards the door.

"Are these photos of your family?" he asked, gesticulating towards the table.

"Yes, most of them," replied Pippa. "I love antique silver, so each time I find another frame for my collection, I have to unearth another photo, and I am running out of good ones. With your Mum it was china, wasn't it?" she asked, adding as she walked across the room, "I'll just switch the fire off before we leave."

"Mum liked her bits of china best," he said, "but she also had an eye for other things and I think I can remember seeing a silver frame somewhere that she discovered at a church jumble sale a few years back. If I find it, I will let you know," he finished generously, as they walked down the stairs and out of the main entrance. They hurried down the footpath to the parking area, buffeted by the wind.

"I'm thinking of redecorating when all the furniture has gone," volunteered Ian holding the car door open for her, his coat flapping against the mirror. She sat down and pulled her coat away from the door as he slammed it shut. Then he struggled round to the driving seat and started the engine.

" I haven't a clue where to start, so I am trying to get some ideas from magazines. I like the colours in your flat," he continued.

"Thanks. It took me ages to decide, there's so much choice these days ... turn right here Ian, it's just down there at the bottom of the road. I can help you with the house if you like. Sometimes it's useful to have someone else's opinion."

"I might take you up on that, I need all the help I can get," he replied gratefully.

It was not a long journey and they soon arrived at the pub car park.

"Will this do?" asked Ian as they drew up into a space.

"This is fine. I can see the band is here – there's the van," she said, pointing to an orange van with blacked out windows that was parked near the door of the pub and with that, Pippa got out of the car and eventually managed to close the door, after a brief tussle with the wind.

They walked into the pub together and could hear the strains of the Beatles' number, 'Revolution', as they entered the warm friendly atmosphere of the Drunken Duck.

It was impossible to talk with the loud music bouncing off the walls, but he worked out that Pippa was asking for a white wine spritzer, which he bought at the bar, together with a glass of orange juice for himself and then they chose a spot and settled down to enjoy the performance. Tim and his three friends were all dressed in baggy jeans and grey long-sleeved T shirts with a stylised holographic 'N' printed on the back. Pippa waved to Tim and he winked at her cheekily.

They played one number after another professionally and with enthusiasm, then the band took a break and leaving his guitar propped up by the microphone, Tim came over to talk to them.

"Glad you came, Pip. What do you think of our set list?"

"I'm really enjoying it actually. Well done. I don't think you know Ian Chisholm do you? He was at North Street Primary, but I think he'd left by the time you started." Tim nodded at Ian.

"Nice to meet you. I hope you are enjoying the music, it is always good to have an unbiased view."

"Yes, I am, you can't beat a live band. How long have you been playing together?"

"Since we all left school actually, but we've only recently started playing on the pub circuit. Sorry, but my friends have got the drinks lined up over there, so if you don't mind I will join them – singing is thirsty work. See you later, Pip," and with that, he walked across to the other side of the bar where the rest of the band were chatting and downing pints of coke or beer.

Ian was actually quite impressed with the band's musical talent. He and Pippa managed a few words along these lines, whilst discussing the pros and cons of pub music, before the band started up again, this time with a song Tim had written himself which went down well, followed by some more old seventies hits, that got several people up on their feet. It was amazing how versatile the band was, he thought and every number was performed so well.

They left the pub just after twelve and Ian drove home trying unsuccessfully, to think of something to say. He wondered what would happen next. He really hoped Pippa would want to see him again – he already thought of her as his girlfriend – but what did she think?

For her part, Pippa was silently cursing her boss, who had signed her up for a course on Italian Ceramics in London for three days the next week. She wouldn't be able to see Ian again until auction day and that seemed ages away.

As they pulled into her road, Pippa was the first one to break the silence.

"I expect you can't wait to see how your Mum's jug does on Friday. I'm on the phone bids this time, so I won't be able to keep you company in the hall."

That was it then. She did not want to see him again. He might have known it was too good to be true. How could he have imagined she would be interested in him, he wondered bitterly. It was a good job he had not mentioned Pippa to his brother, he could just hear the teasing he would have come in for. He felt very stupid to have dared to dream.

"Yes," he said automatically. "Thank you for inviting me to come with you tonight. I enjoyed it."

Did she notice the disappointment in his voice? He hoped not. He didn't want her to think of him as a loser.

The car slowed to a halt and Pippa got out, her scarf blowing in the wind and with a cheery wave, she called out, "See you on Friday," before she opened the main entrance door to her block of flats and went in.

As he drove home, Ian reflected on the evening they had shared and decided he was very fortunate to have been out with her at all. Perhaps sorting out his personal life was going to be much more challenging than he had thought.

On getting out of the car himself a little while later, he noticed that the wind had finally dropped a bit and it was starting to rain quite heavily. Ian hoped his life wasn't going to follow suit. Where on earth did he go from here? He had been given an all too brief glimpse of how his life could be and he realised that he definitely did not want it to revert to how it had been over the past six months or so. He really did not want to be sent back to limbo.

5

Ian lay in bed listening to the rain dripping down from the leaky gutter. Then there was the drone of a distant aeroplane. He tossed and turned and went for a walk around his room. The cathedral clock struck three times. Back in bed again, he wished he could drop off to sleep. He tried to fill his mind with how to paint the front room, but that didn't work either. In desperation, he switched on his bedside radio and tuned it to the World Service. The murmur of voices talking about dentistry in India finally did the trick and he drifted off to sleep.

He awoke to the sound of a choir singing and remembered it was Sunday morning. He decided, on the spur of the moment, to go to church, something he hadn't done for some time, in fact not since his mother's funeral. He felt in need of some spiritual renewal, it was sure to give him a lift. He got out of bed, eased himself into his dressing gown and padded downstairs in his bare feet to get a cup of tea and something to eat.

After breakfast, he quickly washed, shaved and dressed then he peered out of the window. It looked as if the sky was clearing, so he wouldn't have to bother with an umbrella. Fortunately, the church was only half a mile down the road, so it wouldn't take him long to walk there. Actually, it had turned into a very pleasant day. The wind had finally taken its leave and the air was clear and fresh after the rain, the perfect February morning, well almost perfect. It would have been if Pippa had been walking beside him chatting about this and that. He couldn't get her out of his head. Ian straightened his shoulders and told himself there was no point thinking like that now. The church bell started to ring – an *aide memoire* to the faithful that they had five minutes left to get to church before the service started.

St Jude's was a solid red brick Victorian church set in a pretty churchyard. Ian had known it all his life. He and his brother had been baptised and confirmed there, and they had both attended Sunday School too. His parents had both been regular church goers and he could visualise his mother now, singing hymns lustily, if a little off-key and his father handing the collection plate round the congregation. He loved the smell of damp, mixed with beeswax and the scent of flowers that assailed him as he opened the heavy oak doors. It was familiar and comforting.

The organ was playing softly as he collected a service sheet and took his seat at the back of the church, then, all of a sudden the music reached a crescendo, the choir and clergy processed out of the vestry and the service began. It was good to be on autopilot. Ian let the prayers and readings wash over him and nourish his soul. Odd that one of the readings should be full of colour ...

'And the one seated looks like jasper and carnelian, and around the throne is a rainbow that looks like an emerald ...'

Just when he, too, had colours on his mind. Perhaps it was confirmation that he was on the right track. Before he knew it, the organ was playing one last fanfare and the congregation was filing out amidst the murmur of voices and the clatter of teacups. He didn't have time for coffee today, but nodded to some familiar faces and outside the church, shook hands with the vicar and exchanged a few words. He didn't know Fr. Philip very well, but he seemed nice enough and Ian had enjoyed the sermon. Now he would have to hurry if he didn't want to be late for lunch at Mike's house.

Mike and Gaynor lived just outside Linchester in a modern detached house with well-landscaped gardens. They liked Ian to join them for Sunday lunch and this week in particular they all had things to discuss with the auction coming up.

Both their girls were at university, one in Exeter and the other in York, so they only came home in the holidays or for the odd weekend and Gaynor missed them. Ian wasn't great on chit-chat, but he could be very good company in other ways.

Gaynor had always had a soft spot for Ian and did not like the way her husband poked fun at him. He might be a bit boring sometimes, but he had taken a load off their shoulders by doing the lion's share of caring for her late mother-in-law. Her own parents were happily very much alive and kicking.

She just wished he could find a nice partner. The last time he had brought a girl to meet them, Susie and Jane had been quite small. Work seemed to have bogged him down and stressed him out. It was, in her opinion, quite a blessing when he had been made redundant.

She stirred the gravy and looked at everything browning nicely in the oven. Not long now. She hoped he wasn't going to be late.

"Have you opened the wine, Mike?" she called to her husband as he walked past the back door, having been to check out the filter in the ornamental fish pond.

"I'm just about to do it Gaye. I'll wash my hands first though."

At that point there was a knock at the front door and she went off to open it, to find Ian waiting patiently on the doorstep.

"Mm ... something smells good," he smiled appreciatively. She gave him a kiss on the cheek.

"Just a roast chicken with all the trimmings," she replied. "Mike is about somewhere, opening the wine. Come and warm yourself up. At least that awful rain has stopped. What have you been up to?" She asked as she turned to go back and check on her cooking. Ian made some non-committal reply and went off to find his brother, who he tracked down in the office, wrestling with a bottle of Merlot.

As far as brothers went, they had very little in common character-wise, but they looked very much alike with their dark hair and light blue eyes. Ian was a trifle taller and slimmer. Mike was brash and pushy, with a penchant for loud shirts and cowboy boots, quite an extrovert in fact, which was probably due to all the time he spent on building sites, but he was a kind man and for all the teasing was fond of his 'little' brother. Ian on the other hand, was understated – more Rohan meets Ted Baker. Actually Mike rather admired his brother, who had a university degree and several other engineering qualifications, whereas Mike had learnt his trade on the tools. There was six years between them and he took his position as 'head of the family' very seriously.

He had always harboured a secret wish for them to work together on a building project and was hopeful of something suitable turning up soon, now that Ian was free to take up the option. He, too, would have liked to see Ian happily settled in a long-term relationship. He couldn't understand it. His brother had such a lot to offer – and he wasn't getting any younger.

Mike was glad his parents had left their house to Ian. He didn't need it, as he had his own house which he had built himself from scratch and had never particularly liked the old house anyway.

Good luck to him.

"How's it going, mate?" he asked not expecting a reply, then he went on, having finally extricated the cork, "Yes, I know we are having chicken, but I just fancied a bottle of red today."

"Dinner is on the table," called Gaynor from the kitchen and they went through to the dining room in tandem, taking their places at the beautifully laid dinner table and polished off the delicious Sunday lunch of chicken, roast potatoes, carrots, peas, parsnips and stuffing, washed down with the very good red wine, all the time catching up on family gossip, with a bit of sport thrown in. Mike was an avid football fan, and although Ian did not care much about who won or lost, he understood the rudiments of the game and could join in with all the banter but he was more of a cricket and athletics fan himself and had done some marathon running whilst at university. As Gaynor served the apple crumble and cream, the conversation veered round to the auction.

"I have decided to send that old bookcase to the auction, as well as Mum and Dad's bedroom furniture. Hope that's OK with you," started Ian.

"That's fine, I don't want any of that old rubbish. You are doing a great job. The house will look much better without it all. There will be more room too, then you can have us round for Sunday lunch instead," he joked. As an afterthought Mike added, "Any other news?"

This was the question Ian had been dreading. He was a hopeless liar, but he did not want to discuss Pippa. He did not know how. Then, with a flash of inspiration, he saw a way out.

"Yes, I'm going to decorate the house, starting with the lounge. Can you lend me a couple of your painters for a while?"

He was certain this would deflect Mike's interest in him and, sure enough, Mike was happy spending the rest of the time discussing staffing levels, paint finishes and the extortionate cost of decorating materials. Ian was off the hook; well, for this week anyway.

"Let me know when you are ready to start work," said Mike, "I will just need a few days' notice."

Before Ian left, they confirmed their auction arrangements, and agreed to meet outside McFarlanes at ten thirty on Friday. With a bit of luck they would be able to grab a cup of coffee before their lots came up. Once safely on the way home Ian reflected that only suffering a few friendly insults and gaining some colour charts that Mike had found lying round in his office, was a small price to pay for keeping his guilty secret.

6

As he was putting his wheelie bin out for the refuse collection on Monday morning, Ian shivered. He thought there seemed to be more than a hint of snow in the air. He wondered what time the furniture would be collected as he did not want to have to hang around all day; he had several books to return to the library and some other jobs to do. Then he went back inside the house leaving the black wheelie bin outside on the pavement, another sentry standing mutely to attention in line with the others in his road.

He selected a CD from the rack in the sitting room, which subconsciously suited his mood and strode up the stairs to the strains of "Why does it always rain on me ..."

His mother's wardrobe had been emptied months before, but he thought he'd check it one last time. It smelled faintly of her perfume and he suddenly felt his eyes prickle. What was he coming to? He shut the doors roughly and opened a drawer. The lining paper flapped up a bit, but apart from that it was empty. Likewise the others.

He thought that while he was upstairs he would have a look for the photograph frame. Where might his mother have put it? The spare room was his best bet, so he made his way there and opened the door. Immediately he remembered the old leather suitcase stored under the spare bed. He knelt down and pulled it right out into the middle of the floor, then he undid the catch. It smelled of lavender and shut away places, but inside, to his surprise, it was stuffed full of old greetings cards that his mother had obviously carefully saved over the years.

He recognised his own handwriting on a few of them and was moved by her unwillingness to throw them away. On searching further, he discovered some old photographs which meant nothing to him at all, he would have to see if Mike could shed any light on them and finally, hidden away from view in a muslin cloth, the real prize – an ornate silver photograph frame, sadly tarnished.

He removed the frame from its lair, shut the case and shoved it back under the bed to wait for another day when he would have more time to go through the contents thoroughly. Unwilling to mislay the frame again, Ian took it into his bedroom and placed it safely on top of his desk, job done.

Humming along to the music, which was still playing, Ian then walked past the landing window to go downstairs when a flash of red caught his eye. He walked quickly down to the bottom of the stairs and opened the front door. It was as he had thought, there was a van drawing up outside and it was the one he had been expecting from McFarlanes.

"Chisholm?" asked the rather cocky driver, then addressing his elderly companion he said rather impatiently, "Come on Bill, we haven't got all day," and to Ian, "We've come to collect some furniture for the auction on Friday. I'll take the big stuff first, if you don't mind squire." Ian stood aside and ushered them upstairs. It took some time to get the wardrobe out, but eventually, after much grumbling, it was done and the other pieces swiftly followed. Ian took the receipt he was offered for the furniture and sighed as he watched the van drive off. He was just about to shut the door, when a familiar voice hailed him from outside.

"Ian, are you there?" and a tall, well-built man with a startlingly blond beard, appeared on the threshold.

"Garth! It's good to see you," beamed Ian delightedly, " I thought you were in the Sierra Nevada, skiing." Garth Collins had been Ian's best friend at Linchester High School and their firm friendship had stood the test of time. All the new pupils had been seated in alphabetical order on the first day to help the teacher remember their names and Chisholm had shared a desk with Collins.

They clapped each other on the back, with genuine affection.

"I was, I flew back on Saturday," replied his friend. "When I saw that van outside, I thought you'd decided to sell up. What's going on?"

"I have quite a lot tell you, but I don't quite know where to start. Let's have a drink first," said Ian, "is tea all right?"

He explained everything that had happened to him recently over a mug of tea. He even told Garth about Pippa, much to his surprise. Garth listened quietly until he had finished, leaning back in his chair, an inscrutable expression on his face. He rubbed his beard absent-mindedly,

"I think you are being too negative Ian. She sounds lovely and after all, you are going to see her on Friday at the auction. Don't sell yourself short; you are due for a bit of good luck. Tell you what, come round tonight and we will sink a few beers, that will cheer you up."

"I'd love to, but wont Chrissie mind?" asked Ian considerately. Garth's wife, Chrissie had ME. She was often quite low and not up to visitors.

"She will love it, I know. It's ages since you've been round and she is much better these days anyway. While I was away, Chrissie and the twins had a week at her sister's, so she has been filled up with organic veg. and had a nice rest. Besides, she'll probably have some good advice for you about Pippa."

Garth was right about both things. Chrissie was pleased to see Ian and the evening did cheer him up. He left their house feeling much more optimistic and with a determination to make the most of Friday. After all, as Chrissie had pointed out, he hadn't really had much of a chance to build a long-term relationship before as he'd been away for weeks at a time on major road projects, and when he might have done, he was looking after his mother. He and Pippa just needed to get to know each other better.

The following day Ian finally took his books back to the library. It was a modern building conveniently placed in the middle of town and well up on modern technology with several computers for the use of the public, access to the internet, photocopying facilities and friendly, helpful staff.

He exchanged his books for some information on Italy. Perhaps it would help to pass the time and give him something different to think about, especially as the weather continued to be so miserable and he was tired of the seemingly never-ending cold and rain; reading about somewhere warmer might cheer him up he thought.

On the way home, he remembered that he needed some petrol so he made a detour via the Esso garage on the bypass and filled up. While he was waiting to pay, he noticed the display of magazines and newspapers by the door and picked up a newspaper at random, realising that he hadn't seen the news for ages his mind had been so preoccupied. Wondering if he had missed anything of national importance, he removed his card from the machine, took his receipt and drove home.

With the car parked safely in the drive, Ian went inside the house, trying to dodge the raindrops; it would seem he had been wrong about the snow after all, the rain had returned instead, yet again. Settling himself down at the dining room table with a cup of coffee, a ham sandwich and his newspaper, he scanned the headlines and, apart from the usual disasters, people demanding compensation for this and that and political intrigue, he did not think he had missed much. Then as he turned a page, his eye caught the headline:

WOMEN SHUN THE 'MAN WHO HAS IT ALL'

'Some men are just too good to be true, according to a study published today by psychologists' declared the newspaper. 'Surprisingly researchers found that highly attractive men of medium status scored better than highly attractive men of high status' it went on. Ian finished the article, which finally informed the public that women perceived high flyers to be 'less faithful and too good to be true'.

There was hope for him then, he liked it. If he could find a bit of confidence and be himself, he stood a good chance with Pippa. After all, he thought to himself, he was still reasonably good looking, perhaps a few pounds overweight but a bit of exercise would soon sort that out. He was beginning to regain some optimism and he definitely did not want to be thought of as boring any more. By anyone. He would make Pippa see that he was 'highly attractive'. He could do it. He would do it.

7

From that moment on, his outlook on everything changed. He might be a middle-aged orphan, but he still had a life and he was going to live it.

Wednesday dawned bright and breezy, if a trifle cold. After breakfast he collected his swimming shorts from the back of the cupboard, found a towel and threw them into his sports bag, along with some shower gel and a brush, then set off down the road with great purpose. He would not go back home until he had swum at least twenty lengths and been to get a smart haircut.

It was a start and he felt good.

Linchester Eastgate Leisure Centre was about a thirty minute walk away from Ian's house, on the other side of town. It was a typical 1970s concrete edifice, now looking rather tired and stained, but inside the facilities were second-to-none having recently been refurbished. The swimming pool was Olympic size; there was a smaller pool and an enormous flume for those of a more adventurous nature.

As Ian changed out of his clothes and into his swimming shorts, he thought to himself how changing rooms at leisure centres, wherever they might be, inevitably had that humid atmosphere and delicate bouquet of disinfectant mixed with a hint of sweaty feet, which was somehow comfortingly familiar; it always reminded him of school holidays and happy times.

Having chosen a locker and deposited his belongings carefully inside, Ian turned the key in the locker door, slipped the rubber bracelet on his wrist and walked out of the changing rooms, negotiating his way through the showers as he went. He then headed for the sparkling blue waters of the big pool beyond and standing on the side for a moment he hesitated, finally raising his arms above his head and diving in.

He had forgotten how exhilarating swimming could be and the twenty lengths were swiftly accomplished. He managed another two and then heaved himself out. His legs ached a bit, and he felt rather hungry, but apart from that there were no other ill effects. He was surprised he didn't feel more tired, obviously he wasn't as out of shape as he had thought.

Ian luxuriated under a long hot shower and after he was dressed, he decided to treat himself to lunch in the Centre's cafe. He went up to the servery and ordered himself cod and chips with a bottle of water, then balancing the tray in one hand and his sports bag on the other arm, made his way to an empty table and sat himself down to enjoy the food; his fish and chips tasted really good. While he ate, he registered the joyful shrieks of children cascading down the flume in quick succession and watched the swimmers through the large plate glass window separating the spectators from the participators – some just splashing about in the shallow end in their colourful swimsuits and the more serious ones in goggles, relentlessly ploughing their way up and down the pool.

There was a definite feel-good factor about the Leisure Centre and Ian made a mental note to go there more often. Now it was time to carry out part two of his plan. After finishing his lunch, he returned his tray to the counter and walked into town to get his hair cut before he headed for home.

Luckily there was a barber's shop close by and even better, they had some free appointments left. He didn't have to wait too long and when it was his turn, he was ushered over to another part of the shop where he explained to the stylist what he had in mind, then sat down to join in the banal chatter about nights out, holidays and the like, while she worked her magic.

"All done," she declared chirpily as she removed his protective nylon cape in one deft movement, before enquiring, "Is that all right for you?"

Ian looked at himself in the mirror and looking back at him was, he realised with some surprise, someone he hadn't seen for many months. It was someone who took a pride in his appearance, someone with a glint in his eye. Someone in fact who was looking forward with hope.

"Yes, that is just what I wanted, thank you very much," he said smiling happily. "How much do I owe you?"

Back home, Ian watched some television and then put a frozen pizza in the oven for his supper. He decided to give Mike a ring and ask for the painters to start the following week. Now the excess furniture had gone, the front room looked rather bare and somewhat soulless, so he was keen to rearrange things. He wanted the house decorated to his taste as soon as possible, and there was no reason for him to wait any longer.

He dialled the number and waited. It was Mike who picked up the phone,

"Hello Mike," he said.

"Ian? What's up?" asked his brother, surprised to hear his voice.

"Nothing is up exactly, I have just decided I want to make a start on the painting, but just the lounge to begin with."

"That was quick," said Mike, with a laugh, "What colour have you chosen for the walls?"

“I thought pale green would be good and blinds at the windows instead of those awful flowery curtains.”

Mike applauded his choice, made a note of the shade number Ian liked and promised to send his men round on Monday morning to do the work.

“They are finishing off a job for me on Friday, just when we are making our fortunes at the auction of course,” joked Mike.

“Many a true word spoken in jest, Mike. I think you are going to be very surprised,” said Ian. He had high hopes of the jug and he wanted to prove Mike wrong for a change.

His last task for the evening was sorting out the silver frame. He had decided to offer it to Pippa for her collection, but not until it shone like new and had an interesting photograph in it. Phase one of the frame makeover was giving it a good clean up and removing the tarnish caused by years of neglect, so, collecting a soft cloth and an old bottle of silver polish which he had found in the cupboard under the sink in the kitchen, Ian headed upstairs.

8

He was up early on Thursday morning and out for a run. Ian liked all the extra exercise he was doing, it gave him a buzz. He thought three miles would do as a start and had planned a route skirting the city walls. Perhaps he'd stop for a coffee on the way back, then he would ring Garth and see if he was free for lunch.

It was a fairly mild morning, but Ian was taking no chances as the weather had been so fickle of late and he pulled on his black fleece hat and gloves before he set off. As he jogged past the park, the flowerbeds caught his eye. They were a mass of small golden crocuses edged with winter pansies and primula. He thought to himself how hardy these little flowers were and how welcome their colourful blooms appeared coming immediately after the drabness of winter.

It was surprising just how many other people were up and about as early as he was. He noticed some road sweepers at work in the town, then he ran past a couple of other joggers and several walkers with their dogs, not to mention one very large retriever taking his mistress for a brisk trot. Ian liked dogs and had always yearned for one of his own, but having been away so much with work he had never been able to achieve this ambition. Perhaps he would add 'dog' to his wish list – he wondered to himself if Pippa was a dog person.

When he arrived at the coffee bar, some time later, Ian ordered a large Americano and sat down to drink it, but before he could take a mouthful, he heard a voice behind him saying, "Hello, what are you doing here?"

He turned round and for a moment did not recognise the young man sitting there. Then he remembered. It was Tim smiling at him.

Ian immediately smiled back and beckoned him over. "Why don't you come and join me? I don't think I could get up again just yet," he quipped, grimacing and clutching his legs. "I have just been for a run. I didn't have time to tell you how much I enjoyed your playing the other night. Mind you, I was deaf for quite a while afterwards," he went on.

Tim laughed and, picking up his coffee cup, moved across to Ian's table.

"I'm never sure if we sound all right to other people," said Tim a trifle bashfully, "or even if they like the mix of music we have chosen. We are thinking of recording some of our numbers. What do you think?"

"I'm quite sure you are talented enough and some of your original music is outstanding. Actually, I have an old school friend who is a record producer. Would you like me to have a word with him?"

Tim's face lit up. "Another old school friend?" he joked. "But seriously, that would be great."

"Let me have your phone number and I'll do what I can," replied Ian. This casual reference to Pippa pleased him and he watched with a smile, while Tim rummaged through his briefcase. He found one of the posters advertising Nimbus which had his email address printed on it, then he scribbled his mobile number on it as well.

"That should do it. Thanks, Ian, I'm really grateful."

"Don't thank me yet, wait until you see if Garth can help you. By the way, on a completely different tack, does Pippa like dogs?"

"Oh yes! We always had a dog when we were growing up. My Mum is dog mad, and is currently the proud owner of two very lively Lakeland Terrier pups called Nip and Tuck. My father is not so keen, but he puts up with them for a quiet life; actually not that quiet with puppies about. Look, sorry I can't stay and talk more as I am due in court shortly." Tim went on to explain that he was representing a client facing a driving ban.

"Good luck with that and let me know how the music goes."

"Of course I will," called Tim, as he made his way to the door.

He hadn't realised that Tim worked locally, but why would he? Pippa had said he was a solicitor and played guitar in his spare time, but she had not said where he worked. He reckoned someone with Tim's talents deserved a break and Garth was just the man to give him and Nimbus the exposure they needed.

Now he had two reasons to ring Garth, so he picked up his mobile and dialled Garth's number. As usual, it was on answer phone so Ian left him a message, hoping Garth would return his call in time for them to meet for lunch.

He enjoyed the walk back home and was busy rehearsing what he was going to say to Pippa when they next met, when his mobile vibrated in his tracksuit pocket.

"Just returning your call," said Garth.

"Good, just in time. Do you fancy meeting up for lunch? I have a proposition for you."

"Intriguing! I can't wait. How about a Chinese? I'll meet you at the Cross in an hour."

As ever, Garth was the decisive one. Ian agreed and turned his phone off, then he quickened his pace in order to get home, shower and change in time to be back in town for midday. He just made it.

The Market Cross was a mediaeval structure in the middle of Linchester; it had originally been constructed to be used as a woolmarket but was now just a popular meeting place for young and old alike. The stone seats were rather cold and hard, but the young people huddled there did not seem to notice and neither did the two elderly ladies sensibly wrapped up in warm coats and woolly hats surrounded by their shopping bags, who were chatting happily to each other while they waited for their buses.

Garth was already standing there when Ian arrived, and they walked off together anticipating a tasty meal. They chose to eat at the Golden Dragon which was just off the High Street and did a very good sweet and sour pork – a particular favourite of Garth's. Thursday lunchtimes were not usually busy at the Golden Dragon, especially in February, as visitors did not descend on Linchester until Easter, so Ian and Garth had their pick of the tables. They chose one at the back, just behind the enormous model of a Golden Dragon which dominated the room and from which the restaurant took its name. The air was heavy with the aroma of oriental spices, which whetted their appetites and after scrutinising the menu carefully, they made their choices and ordered the food.

"What was it you wanted to discuss with me?" asked Garth with a mouth full of prawn crackers.

"Well, I wondered if you would do me a favour."

"Anything for you. By the way, you seem different, and it's not just your hair. What has happened?"

"Something Chrissie said, plus an article from Tuesday's paper finally made me see things in a new light and I've decided to take myself in hand," said Ian. "Behold the new me!" he added dramatically making a small bow. Garth grinned.

"You don't know how happy I am to hear you say that Ian. Now then, what is this favour? Spit it out."

"Do you remember me telling you about Pippa's brother Tim, who is rather good on guitar? He and some friends have been playing together for a while and when I heard them on Saturday, I thought they were better than the usual chancers you hear at live music gigs, so ..."

"You want me to listen to them."

"In a nutshell, yes. What do you think?"

"I don't see why not. New bands are always welcome. Let me have some contact details and I'll see what I can do."

They finished their leisurely lunch and each found plenty to talk about; it was strange but true, thought Ian to himself, that with really good friends of long-standing however few or many weeks passed in between meetings, once together again roles fall back into familiar grooves. Another of his mother's favourite sayings popped into his head, 'you are given your relations, thank goodness you can choose your friends.' How right she was. Ian gave Garth Tim's contact details and they parted, promising to meet up again very soon.

The rest of the afternoon was taken up with thinking how he should spend his cut of the auction proceeds, always providing of course, that they actually sold anything. Top of Ian's list was a new state-of-the-art laptop computer and perhaps some pictures for the walls of his soon-to-be newly decorated lounge. Then there was Italy.

He picked up one of the books he had borrowed from the library and became engrossed in all things Italian, when he heard the phone ring. He was inclined to leave it. It was probably someone wanting him to change his kitchen, buy a new phone, or even Mark from the recruitment agency who was tenacious in his search for a new job for Ian, even though he had been told numerous times that Ian would contact him when he was ready. In truth, he had been contemplating work over the last few days, but he definitely did not want to work abroad again as he could not bear the idea of leaving Pippa. So, he very nearly did not answer it; but he was extremely glad he changed his mind at the last minute because, as it turned out, it was Pippa herself calling him.

9

The carriage doors hissed open at Linchester station and Pippa disembarked from the train. She had travelled to her course by train because she didn't want to negotiate the M25 in the rush hour, and anyway, there was not much parking available at her hotel, so all in all the train had been a better option.

The course had been much more interesting than she had expected, but she had spent quite a lot of the time daydreaming about Ian. She wondered what was happening in Linchester. She wondered if he had thought about her. It was hard to fathom what he was thinking at any given time, he was so shy and she was going to have her work cut out getting a reaction from him, but she thought it would be well worth it in the end. There was something about him she found irresistible. Pippa promised herself that after she had arrived home, had a bath, washed her hair and unpacked, she would give him a ring. She could quite legitimately ring on the pretext of asking him if everything was in order for Friday's auction, as she had been away from the office for a few days.

Pippa was as good as her thought. She dialled Ian's number and it rang out for such a long time that she was about to put the phone down when she finally heard his voice.

"Hi, it's Pippa. I just thought I'd ring to see if you are all ready for tomorrow."

The new Ian sprung into action, and answered Pippa with, "Yes, I am thanks. I'm glad you called because I wanted to run a couple of things past you. I think I'll have pale green on the sitting room walls, and what do you think about blinds instead of curtains? Apparently

John Lewis has a good selection of blinds. Perhaps we could go and see on Saturday? Look, I'll give you my mobile number now, in case you need to get in touch when I am out and about."

There, he had done it; he had willed himself out of his self-imposed inertia and had now embarked on the cruise of his life, hopefully with Pippa by his side. He couldn't wait to see where it might take him and what new experiences awaited him.

Pippa had never heard him make such a long speech before and was flattered that he rated her advice so highly, "I think green is a very relaxing colour, Ian, especially very pale green. I'd love to go to John Lewis with you. I don't often get over there as it is such a long trek, but I know they are very good in the home furnishings department. Saturday is fine by me."

At last he had given her his mobile phone number and she felt excited at the prospect of spending a day in his company. Perhaps she would be able to get him to open up a bit more, she was absolutely certain their friendship was destined to blossom.

When he eventually put the phone down, Ian's head was in a spin, but he was very pleased with his new proactive stance. Pippa had explained to him about the course she'd just finished. After her initial reluctance, she had really enjoyed it. Italian Ceramics was a fascinating subject. She was looking forward to seeing him the next day and meeting his brother too.

So what was he to make of all that? She had phoned him, and she hadn't wanted to finish the conversation either. Things were looking up and he couldn't help smiling to himself. He was really optimistic about Friday now, from all aspects. He didn't have long to wait, and on that happy thought he turned the lights out and went up to bed.

For the first time in a few days, Ian slept well, he thought it must be all the exercise he was doing. Nevertheless, he woke early and decided he just had time for a quick run before breakfast, as he did not want his regime to slip.

The sky was overcast, but it wasn't raining thank goodness. He knew his furniture would go under the hammer outside and it would be a pity if it got wet before it was sold. His route took him down to the canal and along the towpath for a bit. His father had often taken him down there as a child to look for frogspawn and do a bit of fishing.

The canal was deserted, apart from the moorhens flapping about in the reeds and some swans floating effortlessly up and down in the water, preening themselves from time to time. Ian thought how majestic the swans looked, especially with their little family of cygnets in tow, rather like a royal entourage with pageboys following on behind. All he could hear was the faint hum of traffic from the bypass and some seagulls calling to one another from nearby rooftops. He was thinking about Italy, Florence in particular.

Should he chance his luck and ask Pippa to join him on a short holiday? Definitely worth a try, if only he could pluck up the courage from somewhere. Worst case scenario, she would be 'too busy' and preferred option, she would jump at the chance. The latter was a very satisfying thought.

Now he had run far enough, so he turned for home, neatly sidestepping a puddle on the muddy towpath and startling a blackbird, sending it complaining into the undergrowth. Linchester was beginning to wake up. Ivy Ellison from next door was coming out of her gate as he jogged along towards his house.

"Hello love," she called, pulling her gate behind her and making the latch rattle. "Nice to see you keeping fit. I'm just off to get my newspaper. I noticed the van the other day. Got rid of a few bits and pieces did you? Have they gone to McFarlanes? Quite right," she answered her own question.

She had known Ian since he was a little boy and he knew her interest was kindly meant. When he could get a word in, he replied, "Morning Mrs E. Yes, just trying to make a bit more room. I'll be redecorating too, and when I have, you can come over for a cup of tea."

Mrs Ellison beamed with pleasure. "Try keeping me away," she said and with a little wave of her battered old purse, she walked slowly into town, doing up her coat as she went.

Ian let himself into the house and put the kettle on. He would have his breakfast, then get ready for the day ahead. There was a knot of excitement in his stomach, but he was not going to let the new optimism and confidence he had found, desert him. Things could only get better.

10

James McFarlane loved auction days. Even after all this time – forty years come May – he still felt the same excitement at the unpredictability of the day ahead and he could not wait to take his turn with the gavel. He drove into the auction yard and parked his car out of the way, so as not to interfere with the setting-up.

It was still early, but the porters were already busy lining up the furniture. They were bringing out boxes of pictures, old books, mixed china and then row upon row of old chairs, mirrors and tables that had been stored in the sheds adjacent to the yard. If the rain kept off, they would be lucky, he thought to himself, glancing up at the overcast sky, then he let himself into the hall which was now looking like Aladdin's cave.

His experienced eye scanned the assorted paraphernalia with satisfaction and he eagerly inhaled the evocative bouquet of old books and polished wood. There were several display cabinets, some filled with assorted silverware, some with expensive pieces of china and some with antique and second-hand jewellery, not to mention old pens, fans and sets of medals. A slightly battered suit of armour stood dejectedly by the entrance to the yard, and two longcase clocks, either side of the office door. The Toby jugs Ian had noticed on his first visit to McFarlanes, had been joined on the shelf by a pair of china dolls in embroidered silk dresses, three train sets, a couple of model steam engines and a solitary violin in a velvet-lined case.

The walls were covered with oil paintings, large and small, numerous rather faded watercolours and a few Victorian prints in elaborate frames. The mahogany table groaned under the weight of cut and coloured glass objects, decorative ceramics, miscellaneous cutlery and stylish photograph frames.

In the corner, was an old brass adjustable standard lamp on a Grecian column with a square base and paw feet, flanked by two elegant chandeliers and adding a splash of colour were some stuffed birds with lurid plumage laced with dust, half a dozen Chinese floral rugs and that very fine Clarice Cliff jug. Feeling quite pleased with himself and full of anticipation for a successful auction to come, James walked across the echoing floorboards and through to the hub of his little empire.

Pippa was already there; in fact she had arrived before eight. He had high hopes of her and what is more, thought she added a touch of class to McFarlane & Sons. When he had taken her on, the old guard of auctioneers had been very scathing about him employing a 'young bit of a girl', but James had seen her potential and to his credit, he had been proved right. In fact he was considering offering her a partnership in the firm over the next few months he was so pleased with her progress. That would mean he could back pedal a bit, which would make his wife very happy.

"Pippa!" he declared cheerily.

"Morning James. It looks like the rain is holding off."

"You are on phone bids today aren't you, Pippa?"

"Yes, that's right. There has been quite a lot of interest in that Clarice Cliff jug you know. It could go sky high."

"Let's hope so. It's been a long time since we have had such a good example. Actually there are several first rate lots this month, I can't wait to get started. Is Beth here? I could do with a coffee before everything kicks off," and with that he disappeared into his room. Beth arrived on cue, slightly flustered.

"The buses are all to pot this morning and just when I wanted to get ahead of myself. Auction days are always pandemonium," she complained. Pippa laughed and passed on James's message. Beth switched on the computer, "I'll put my bag away, then I'll fetch Mr McFarlane his coffee. Do you want one too?" she asked.

"Yes please, I'll just be outside," replied Pippa looking at her watch. Only ten minutes to go before she could unlock the front doors then she knew she wouldn't stop until the auction ended. Ian's first items weren't up until about eleven o'clock and the jug, being Lot number 387, not until early afternoon. She went off to check the outside lots one more time.

Mike arrived ten minutes before Ian and joined the crowd of bidders watching the sale. The auctioneer's voice boomed out, "Lot number 56. An oak corner cupboard. Now, shall we say twenty pounds for this? Who'll start me at twenty? Ten then, surely someone will give me ten? Thank you sir, I have ten. Fifteen anywhere? Fifteen. Twenty? I have twenty pounds. Twenty-five? ..."

"You got here early, Mike." Mike hadn't noticed Ian coming up behind him he was so fascinated by everything and he turned round in surprise.

"Hello, yes, didn't want to be late." Then he added, "There are lots of punters here. Let's hope they are feeling generous today. I haven't seen our furniture though, there's such a lot of other stuff. It's much bigger than I had imagined. I thought I'd wait for you to get here before I bought a catalogue."

"No need, they posted me one. I've got it here. Our Lots are 79, 80, 83, 84, 230 and 387. Do you want to have a look?" and Ian held out the pamphlet. Mike took it and thumbed through it quickly, while Ian surveyed the scene. He could see the furniture on the far side of the yard, and he pointed it out to Mike, but there was no sign of Pippa.

The auctioneer was up to Lot 60 now – he didn't waste any time. Just a few more Lots, then it would be theirs.

Coffee would have to wait until the furniture had gone under the hammer.

"Lot 79. Mahogany bedroom suite" Ian was holding his breath. What was that? A hundred and fifty pounds already. No, it was a hundred and sixty and the hammer went down. The bookcase was next. That went for an amazing three hundred pounds; two more lots, then the two tables and finally the chairs. Mike had a big grin on his face. So far they had netted six hundred and twenty pounds. Pippa had been very close with her estimate. Now they could go inside the hall and have a browse around before the jug had its five minutes of fame.

"That went well," chortled a delighted Mike. "Shall we go inside now and have a look at everything else? How long have we got before the china?"

"About an hour I think. There is a cafe over the road, let's get a drink first, all this excitement is making me thirsty."

11

Meanwhile, Pippa was busy in the office checking through the records, helping Beth with payments and handing out bidding numbers. They always employed extra staff to help on auction days and people were continually filing in and out of the office. She wondered if she would have a chance to talk to Ian before the phone bidding started. Where was he? Surely he'd arrived by now.

Ian and Mike returned to McFarlanes, refreshed and were soon back in the hall, deciding what to look at first. Mike took a fancy to the stuffed birds and made his way across the room to examine them. Ian scanned the pictures briefly, then he noticed the longcase clocks and went over to have a better look. Suddenly Mike was beside him, prodding him in the arm.

"Never mind those grandfather clocks, look at that! She's a bit of all right. Over there Ian, watch it, she's coming our way." Ian turned round to see what Mike was talking about and found himself looking straight into Pippa's eyes.

She smiled at him and his heart leapt.

"Ian, there you are. I wondered where you'd got to."

Mike's face was a picture. How could Ian possibly be on first name terms with such a stunner? Ian pulled himself together.

"Hello Pippa. We've been here a while, but just popped out for a drink. It's all very exciting. This is my brother Mike. Mike, Pippa."

"Nice to meet you. My brother is a dark horse; where has he been hiding you?" Trust Mike to try and embarrass him, but Ian had recovered now, and ignoring Mike he went on, "The furniture went well. Six hundred and twenty pounds. We are hoping our china is as successful. There seem to be a lot of bidders here today."

"I'm glad you are pleased. I thought it would all sell, but you can never tell until the day. There is a good turnout and we have had several enquiries about that jug. Now we put the catalogue on our website, we can reach a much larger audience and hopefully get a better price for our lots."

Mike for once, had nothing to say. He was still getting over the shock of Ian having a 'secret life'. What else didn't he know? He was not used to this at all.

"Have you had a good look round?" enquired Pippa, "We'll be starting in the hall very soon and then it will be impossible to move about much."

"I think we have seen enough, haven't we Mike? We'll just find a seat and settle down to watch."

Mike nodded and followed Ian meekly. What on earth was going on?

Pippa went off to answer a bidder's question, thinking to herself that Ian was even better looking than she had remembered and the two brothers sat down in the only two vacant seats. It was amazing how quickly they had filled up now the outside bidding was finished and there was a steady stream of people filtering in to take their place in the hall.

"Where in goodness' name did you meet her?" asked a bewildered Mike, *sotto voce*.

"She came to the house to value the furniture and we discovered we had both been at North Street Primary at the same time," said Ian quietly but confidently. "She is lovely, isn't she," he added rather dreamily.

"Something has happened to you," replied Mike, with grudging respect. "You are really coming out of your shell."

"Shh," hissed Ian. "He's about to start."

James McFarlane walked up to the rostrum, took a sip of water from the glass in front of him, and surveyed the room. He noted that as well as the usual suspects, the room contained a fair number of new faces as well, which was good. He was pleased to see such a big turnout, it should be a profitable month. He felt the adrenalin rise and addressed the room.

"Right, ladies and gentlemen, shall we start? Lot 220, an apothecary's cabinet complete with glass bottles. Shall we say fifty pounds for this? Fifty pounds I have. Fifty-five, sixty, sixty-five, seventy." Mike was beginning to glaze over, but when the auctioneer said, "Ah a new bidder," he started to take notice again.

"One hundred and thirty, one hundred and forty. I have one hundred and forty ... Are you all finished? Going once, one hundred and forty twice, sold at one hundred and forty pounds to the gentleman at the back. Number please? Thank you. Lot 221, an old French brass carriage clock ..."

"Keep your hands still, Mike," whispered Ian, "we don't want to end up buying something."

"Sorry, but these chairs are a bit hard. Only nine more before Mum's bits and pieces, then the jug. I just can't sit still."

"Well, you will have to. I think Pippa is helping with the next one, she's standing by the phone now."

Sure enough, Pippa was bidding for a client determined to buy a Georgian Serpentine chest. The bidding finished at one thousand five hundred and fifty pounds and then they heard ...

"Lot 230, a carton of assorted decorative china. Who will give me thirty pounds for this lot? ..Twenty then? Twenty pounds over there. Twenty, twenty-five, thirty, thirty-five, forty, forty-five. Any advance on forty-five? Fifty pounds, thank you. Fifty-five? Fifty-five, sixty. I have sixty pounds once, twice, sold. Your number please, madam?

"Not quite up to estimate," said Ian in Mike's ear.

"Better than nothing though," retorted Mike. "It's the jug I'm interested in."

At last they heard the number they were waiting for.

"Lot number 387. A very fine example of a Clarice Cliff jug, fully marked. Great interest in this item, I can start the bidding at two thousand pounds." The hall went quiet and Ian noticed that there were two porters holding telephones, as well as Pippa. The bidding bounced backwards and forwards. It went swiftly past four thousand five hundred, then up to five thousand five hundred, leaving Ian and Mike on tenterhooks.

James was really enjoying himself, "I have five thousand five hundred pounds are there any more bids?" he asked, looking in the direction of the telephones. Pippa, gripping the phone tightly, spoke quietly to the client on the other end, then looking at James, she shook her head. The other two porters also conferred with their clients.

"Six thousand pounds?" asked James. "Right, I have six thousand pounds. I'm selling at six thousand pounds, once. No, six thousand five hundred. I have six thousand five hundred pounds, going once, going twice, sold, on the phone at six thousand five hundred pounds," he declared triumphantly, and banged the gavel down with a flourish.

In that instant, the whole room came back to life again, papers rustled, people got up and walked about, James called the next Lot and Ian and Mike looked at each other, completely shocked. Mike was the first to recover.

"Well, that's it then. Let's go back outside," and he gave Ian a friendly push towards the door.

Outside, the yard was almost deserted. Just the odd cardboard box and lonely item of uncollected furniture left to greet them. The weather had taken a turn for the worse, and raindrops pierced the little puddles where the tarmac had been worn away over the years. Oblivious to all this, Mike danced a crazy jig

"Thank you Mum," he said, rather too loudly for Ian's liking, "the old girl obviously knew a thing or two. I must go and tell Gaye the news then I have to pick Susie up from the station. She's home from Exeter for the weekend, so I'd better get on, but we have to celebrate. How about a drink tonight? Even better, we could have Sunday lunch at Le Vignot for a change. What do you think?"

Ian was actually thinking that it was a shame his mother was not there to celebrate with them, but did not want to say so, because he knew Mike would tell him not to be so daft, so he merely replied, "Why not, give me a ring later. I'm going back inside to check what happens next, and ask Pippa if there's any more paperwork to sort out," congratulating himself on finding another excuse to speak to Pippa.

"Fine, speak to you later. Get in there." and with a conspiratorial wink, Mike hurried off to find his car.

Gaynor had been taking advantage of Mike's absence at the auction to give his office a thorough clean. She usually only managed a perfunctory whizz round with the hoover each week, but a rogue ray of sunlight when she was passing the door made her see just how dusty and untidy it was in there and she was glad to have found something to do to pass the time while she waited for news.

Having rationalised the piles of papers, trade magazines and catalogues, she reorganised his heap of samples and dusted the blinds and shelves. Then she cleaned the window and computer screen and polished his desk until it shone. Finally satisfied with all her efforts, she shut the door and went to wash her hands. She was just drying them, when she heard Mike's key in the lock.

"Gaye, are you in?" she went to the kitchen door still holding the towel, but before she could reply, Mike blurted out the news about the jug,

"It went for six thousand five hundred pounds! Can you believe someone actually paid six thousand five hundred pounds for that funny old jug?"

"I thought you looked pleased with yourself. What about the other things?" she asked excitedly.

"Everything went. I think we made over seven thousand altogether, but I have got something even more surprising and exciting to tell you, Gaye. You will never guess what."

"You got a parking ticket?" suggested Gaynor frivolously. He shook his head.

"Well, I don't know, just tell me."

"He's got a girlfriend. Ian has found himself a girl, and what a girl. You just have to meet her Gaye, her name is Pippa. I thought we could all get together to celebrate on Sunday – go out for lunch for a change."

"Really? I'm so pleased, Mike. Who is she, what does she do? What does she look like? Where did you meet her? Where did Ian meet her?" Gaynor fired off her questions in quick succession.

"Put the kettle on, I'm parched," pleaded Mike. "Phew, what an afternoon. I'll tell you everything, but I mustn't be too long, don't forget I have to meet Susie in half an hour."

Mike relayed his information while Gaynor made him a mug of tea. She had to interrupt him a few times to fill in the bare bones he gave her, but eventually she had heard enough and Mike managed to gulp down his tea.

"I'll have to go now, just look at the time," and kissing her hastily on the cheek he left for the station.

By herself once more, Gaynor had time to think about the startling news Mike had just given her.

Fancy Ian surprising them. It was good he had finally decided to change things in the old house. She and Mike had thought for a long time that he should move on in his life, but how to persuade him so to do had often been the topic of their nocturnal ruminations. Now it seemed they had underestimated him and Ian had not needed their help after all. He was doing all right on his own, better than all right. Never had they imagined he had been hiding a girlfriend in the wings.

She was genuinely delighted for him and lunch out was a great idea. Susie would be there too, which was a bonus as she got on well with her uncle. If anyone could coax him out of his shell she could and she would also be the perfect icebreaker with Pippa. How could it fail to be a lively and enjoyable gathering? Sunday, she decided, was going to be great fun.

12

Back in the auction hall meanwhile, Ian was thinking the exact opposite. Would it be a good idea to inflict a family Sunday lunch on Pippa so soon? Could *he* cope with it? Mike would be bound to put his foot in it somehow. The only spark of hope for an enjoyable time was that Susie would be joining the party. He liked Susie. She made him laugh and amazingly had always been interested in what he had to say. She was bound to get on with Pippa as she was a real people person and perhaps she would be able to deflect some of her father's black humour. Anyway, Pippa knew nothing of these plans yet. He could be worrying about nothing, Pippa could have her own plans for Sunday.

The auction was slowly tailing off. There were only a few bidders left in the hall and Pippa had returned to the office. Ian walked through to join her and waited his turn behind several people who were settling their bills and collecting the items they had just bought.

"Ah, Mr Chisholm," she said with feigned reverence, "what can I do for you?"

"I just came to check that I hadn't forgotten to sign something, and to thank you for all your help," he began, "never having sold at auction before, I'm not sure what happens next."

Pippa explained about the commission to be paid and that Ian would receive a cheque from McFarlanes within the next two weeks.

"Are you in a hurry to go?" she asked. "If not, we could have a chat about everything when I finish up here." Ian agreed to wait and went to find a seat in the hall. It wasn't long before she joined him. He thought she looked a bit tired.

"What a pleasure to sit down. My feet are killing me. Well, what did you think about your first auction Ian?"

"It was a real eye-opener," he replied, "Mike and I both found it riveting. The suspense with the bidding over the jug was something else. I'm sure my Mum would have loved every minute even though she had never been to an auction before either and she found the idea of auctions rather daunting. She loved going to the theatre though, and auctions seem to me to be a variation on the theatrical theme. I suppose you could call them old-time Music Halls with the Lots as star turns and the auctioneer as Master of Ceremonies."

"I suppose you are right," said Pippa, smiling, " I had never thought of it quite like that myself, but some auctioneers I know are very theatrical, especially in the way they dress!"

His own enthusiasm surprised him and he suddenly realised that going home to his quiet, empty house held no appeal at all. Buoyed up by his positive auction experience, Ian went on bravely, " I don't feel like going home now. I don't suppose you would like to come to the cinema with me instead?" Somehow she made it all so simple.

The idea of sitting down for a couple of hours appealed to Pippa a great deal, apart from which she was very attracted to Ian and wanted to get to know him better, so she agreed straight away.

"I'll go and fetch my things, I will be back in a minute," she replied.

Oh no! Watching her walking off reminded Ian that he hadn't brought his car with him. He knew he would have had trouble parking, so he had left it at home and had come to the auction on foot. What a fool he was. Pippa was going to think him a complete idiot.

"Right, I'm ready now." She was back in next to no time.

"Er ... slight problem. I didn't bring my car this morning," apologised Ian, rather red-faced.

"Don't worry, that's fine. Mine is parked at the back. Actually, if you had brought yours, it would have made things more complicated. Shall we go?"

Ian marvelled at the way she always made him feel at ease and from feeling an idiot one minute, he felt on top of the world the next. How did she do that? And he followed her out into the yard.

The multiplex cinema was on the outskirts of Linchester, along with some fast food outlets and a bowling alley. It was only two years old and had a wide variety of choice in the films shown and snacks available. They both wanted to see the latest James Bond movie, so that decision was easy, but they agreed to differ over the snacks. Pippa decided on a bag of popcorn and a bottle of water, while Ian chose a hot dog and coke. Armed with their provisions, they sauntered over to the correct queue.

"Only half an hour to go now," remarked Ian between mouthfuls.

"We timed it nicely then," said Pippa who was only picking at her popcorn as she wanted it to last. Eventually they filed in and it wasn't long before the familiar theme tune boomed out across the cinema.

The rain had started in earnest while they were watching the film and going outside again brought them back to earth with a bump. Ian grabbed Pippa's hand

and they ran over to the car, giggling like schoolchildren as they went. While Pippa was fastening her seatbelt, she asked Ian about their trip to John Lewis the next day, then she started the engine. Ian had already thought about this and was ready with his reply.

"We will go in my car tomorrow. I'd like to leave quite early, then we can have a good look round. How would it be if I collected you at nine?" Before she had time to comment on this, he added, "Actually I was wondering if you would like to join us for lunch on Sunday. I usually go to Mike's house, but this week we thought we would celebrate our auction success at Le Vignot."

Ian held his breath, but he had no need to worry because, unknown to him, Pippa loved French cuisine and she was not going to pass over an invitation to Le Vignot, by far the best restaurant in Linchester. Apart from that, the more she saw of Ian, the more she liked him.

"That sounds perfect," she said negotiating the roundabout outside the cinema complex and Ian breathed easily again. When eventually she stopped the car outside his house, Pippa wondered if he was going to kiss her goodnight. In the next second, she decided to leave nothing to chance and thought she would kiss him herself so she leant across towards him, saying,

"Goodnight Ian, see you tomorrow," and planted a kiss on his cheek. He responded with a lingering kiss on her lips and in that moment, they both knew for sure that their relationship was destined to be more than that of two old school friends.

13

"What is he playing at?" asked Mike peevishly. "I tried him twice last night and again just now, but he is not answering the landline and his mobile is switched off."

"He is probably having a lie-in," replied Gaynor soothingly, "try again in half an hour."

"Morning Marge!" Gaynor's face lit up. It was Susie, up and about before ten o'clock which was quite unheard of. Gaynor loved it when Susie used her pet name. It came from the nursery rhyme days when she had bounced the girls on her knees and sung Margery Daw to them, while they squealed in delight. Susie had her mother's straight fair hair and her father's blue eyes. She was taller than Gaynor and very slim. Wrapped up in an oversize bathrobe however, she looked just like a little girl again.

"Any toast going?" she asked.

"Don't call your mother that ridiculous name," said Mike with mock severity, "what is the matter with 'Mum'?"

"I don't mind Mike, leave her alone. Come and sit down dear. Do you want cereal first?"

Susie nodded and a strand of hair fell across her sleepy face but she brushed it aside with a delicate flick of her wrist.

"Were you talking about Uncle Ian? Perhaps he's out with his girlfriend," suggested Susie helpfully, and to her mother who handed her a bowl of Cornflakes, "Thanks Marge, I'll just get a spoon."

"There you are, Mike, that's probably exactly where he is. Send him a text message instead. You can always book a table for the three of us and then alter the numbers later."

Placated, and seeing the logic in this, Mike headed off to his newly spruced up office to sort it out.

"Shall we go shopping this morning?" wheedled Susie, "I've only brought a few clothes with me and nothing smart enough for Le Vignot."

This was music to Gaynor's ears. She had been having a tussle with her conscience as to whether a new dress was justified or not. Of course it was. Mike would pay, as she knew he had just banked some money from a recent house sale, and she had a hunch there was another project in the pipeline, although Mike was keeping very quiet about it at the moment. As business was so good there was no reason why she and Susie could not spend some money and have quality time together choosing something for them both to wear on Sunday.

"I'll just tell Dad what we're doing, and we'll go as soon as you are ready. I love it when you come home, Susie, you add a bit of sparkle to the place," she called as she practically skipped down the passageway and into the office.

Susie found it impossible to hurry anywhere, a habit which particularly infuriated her father and it was some time before she was completely ready to leave and hardly morning at all, but finally she and Gaynor set off for the shops.

Linchester had a good selection of clothes shops, from national chains to bijou boutiques; Gaynor loved a bargain and the phrase 'twenty per cent off' reeled her in every time. The January sales lingered in most of the shops and she was confident that they would have no difficulty finding suitable outfits at a reasonable price.

Susie saw some black trousers she liked in the first shop they tried; they were very much like all her others Gaynor thought, but she smiled indulgently and said how nice they were.

"No," said Susie emphatically, "I can't buy the first thing I see. Let's try over the road."

They crossed the road and visited three more trendy shops, full of teenagers with skinny legs, dangly earrings and multicoloured hair, but Susie, although thorough in her search, could not find anything she liked. A long-suffering Gaynor suggested the big department store just opposite the cathedral, and off they went in that direction.

She was sure they would find a dress for her without too much trouble and as this store catered for the younger age group too, she was quite optimistic. Even luckier, to her delight, when they walked past the enormous display windows at the front of the store, she read

'Just One Day – CLOTHING UP TO 70% OFF.'

"We are bound to find something here, Marge, just up your street," chuckled Susie.

Gaynor's eyes gleamed as they walked through the automatic doors and up the escalator.

As predicted, there were several outfits that took Gaynor's fancy and, wonder of wonders, Susie found a top in an electric blue she really loved, which fitted her perfectly. She then helped Gaynor with her choice and insisted on her mother trying on two skirts, one dress and a very smart grey silk suit.

The suit won, hands down on price, fit and shade, and so did a jumper that had nothing to do with Sunday, but Gaynor just liked the colour.

They took their purchases to the till and Susie finally decided she'd like to buy the trousers from the first shop after all, so when Gaynor had settled the bill, off they trailed back again, tired but both equally pleased with their afternoon's work.

14

Susie was right of course, Ian was out with Pippa. In fact he was busy doing much the same things as his niece, but at John Lewis instead.

The nearest branch was an hour's drive away, but it was well worth the journey as it was a megastore on three floors with a restaurant at the top, providing panoramic views of the surrounding countryside. They planned to have their lunch there and return to Linchester late afternoon.

The day had been a great success and they returned to Ian's house laden with carrier bags. It was only when Ian got inside and checked his messages that he realised he hadn't let Mike know yet if he and Pippa would be joining the party at Le Vignot. He rang Mike straight away.

"Sorry mate, I've been out shopping with Pippa. We are both coming tomorrow. I hope we haven't left it too late to let you know."

"No, that's fine. I've booked a table for one o'clock and said I would confirm numbers this evening. Shall we meet for drinks beforehand?"

"OK. We'll be there at about half past twelve then. See you tomorrow." And before Mike could ask him any embarrassing questions, Ian put the phone down.

Pippa was waiting patiently for him in the sitting room, trying to visualise the planned improvements in her mind's eye. With her help, Ian had bought some new cushions, a rug to put in the middle of the floor and blinds in a complimentary shade. It should come together nicely, she thought approvingly.

They had decided to go and have supper at Pippa's flat as she had some salmon in her fridge which they could share. After all, she wasn't going to need it for her lunch on Sunday. To her, this was the perfect end to a perfect day.

Ian popped his head round the door.

"I'll just fetch a bottle of wine from the garage, for us to have with our meal, then we can go. I won't be long."

Pippa stood up, picked up her bag, shrugged her coat over her shoulders and walked into the hall. She noticed a pile of books stacked neatly against the wall and wondered what Ian was planning to do with them. He was certainly taking his clean sweep seriously.

She peeped into the kitchen and quickly took in the tired decorations and worn floor covering. The cupboards had attractive pine doors which were in good condition and there were plenty of them, so it wasn't all bad news, and standing rather forlornly next to the back door, was the pine dresser recently denuded of its china. She wondered if Ian was planning to do this room next.

Everywhere seemed clean, but dated and now Ian had made a start, she could encourage him with the rest. It would be fun helping him, especially as it would mean their spending more time together.

Sunday lunch sounded like fun too. Le Vignot was one of her favourite restaurants and you could guarantee a good meal every time. It had once been a grand family house and the interior was superb with polished wood panelling and ornate plasterwork. Pippa particularly liked the fluffy white towels in the ladies' cloakroom. This train of thought led her to thinking about Gaynor and Susie. What were they like? Mike seemed quite sweet, but he certainly rubbed Ian up the wrong way. At this point, Ian returned with his bottle of wine and put an end to her musings.

"Right, now we can go. I had trouble getting past some of the boxes in the garage – I really must tackle that next," he said unknowingly answering her unasked question. "I wonder how I ever found the time to work," he joked. "Do you know, I am quite looking forward to tomorrow now I've got you to keep me company. I just hope Mike behaves himself."

"Don't worry," answered Pippa gamely, "I'm sure we'll cope," and she put her arm through his as they walked out of the house.

15

Sunday dawned wild and blustery. The sun was making a valiant attempt to appear, but scudding grey clouds fought with the blue sky and won. It was only a matter of time before the rain would be back.

Ian was up by nine and out for one of his runs, then on his return he showered and put on the new shirt Pippa had chosen for him the day before at John Lewis. It was a heavy cotton weave with alternate thick blue and white stripes and although not his usual style, he liked it. He wanted to be ready in good time so that he could go and buy her some flowers as a thank you for all her help.

Pippa, too was taking great care over her appearance. She wanted to make a good impression on Ian's family. It was a toss up between her smart black trouser suit, or a swishy knee-length cream dress with a green and black swirly pattern on it. She eventually decided on the dress and she wore it with her favourite black suede boots and some stunning jet earrings. She decided to leave her hair loose as she had just washed it, now all she had to do was apply some mascara and a touch of lip gloss.

"*Voilà*!" she said out loud to her reflection in the mirror, "Le Vignot, here I come."

Then she went into the sitting room to wait for Ian.

He arrived at her flat just before twelve, and armed with an enormous bunch of scented lilies, rang the bell. Pippa answered the door quickly.

"Ian, they are lovely, thank you. Mmm," and she buried her nose in the fragrant blooms. "Come in for a minute while I put them in water. By the way, that shirt looks great on you."

Ian walked into the flat and closed the door behind him.

"I wanted to say 'thank you' for everything, Pippa. I really appreciate all the time you have spent helping me and I have really enjoyed all the time I've spent with you. The last few days have meant a lot to me."

She left the lilies in a large bowl of water and put her arms around him, saying spiritedly,

"I have really enjoyed myself, too. It's a shame we didn't get to know each other better at school. Never mind, we can make up for lost time now. You're not feeling nervous about lunch are you?"

"Not as much as I thought I would, but we had better get off soon though, or we'll be late." Ian gently disengaged himself from her arms and gave her a kiss on the top of her head, savouring the perfume that wafted about as she moved.

They walked out to the car and Pippa told him that Tim had left a cryptic message on her answerphone about Garth and Nimbus, but she couldn't quite make it out.

"I'm glad Garth has made contact, I wonder what it is all about?" said Ian. "I'll ring him later and find out."

Mike was feeling quite pleased with himself; Gaynor and Susie were both ready on time and his little branch of the family had arrived at Le Vignot first. His only small pang of regret was the absence of Jane. He had spoken to her on the phone of course, but it wasn't quite the same. He had promised to get some pictures of Pippa to send her later and had his digital camera neatly stashed away in his jacket pocket for just that purpose.

The waiter came over with a tray of drinks and brought the menu with him.

"May I see, Dad?" asked Susie," it will be good to have a decent meal for a change. I only ever eat pasta at uni."

"You had a decent meal last night – there is nothing wrong with Mum's cooking." chided Mike then, "Gaye!" he added breathlessly, "they're here."

Three pairs of eyes turned towards the door. Ian and Pippa were walking over towards them, hand in hand.

Susie stood up smiling, "Hello Uncle Ian. Smart haircut and I love that shirt."

"You don't look so bad yourself pipsqueak," he replied with a smile and gave her a hug. "This is Pippa everybody."

"Hi, Pippa," said Susie casually,

Gaynor and Mike were both standing up now and said simultaneously, "Pleased to meet you," and "Hello again," then Mike went on, "What would you both like? Drinks are on me."

Ian ordered an orange juice, as he was driving and wanted a glass of wine with the meal and Pippa thought she would have a gin and tonic. Mike dashed off to the bar and Gaynor suggested they all sit down again.

"How did you two get on with your shopping yesterday?" she asked.

Pippa replied for both of them, "Very well, thanks. We did our best to empty John Lewis. I think Ian has had some really good ideas with his redecoration scheme."

"I didn't know you were going to do some painting Uncle Ian. What a shame I have to go back to Exeter tomorrow, I could have helped you," exclaimed Susie with a twinkle in her eye.

"I'm not doing the painting myself, I'm borrowing a couple of your Dad's painters and even if I were, I would not ask you to help. Remember last time?" This was in reference to Susie's efforts at decorating her own bedroom, when a tin of paint somehow, unaccountably, got spilt all over the window.

"Ha, ha! Anyway, tell me what you are going to do with your auction money."

"Susie, enough. Uncle Ian's money is his own business. They did do very well on Friday though, didn't they Pippa?"

"Are you talking about the auction?" asked Mike who had returned from the bar.

"The waiter will be here in a minute with your drinks. How much money did we make in the end?"

"After commission and VAT the total was five thousand nine hundred and fourteen pounds and fifty-three pence," declared Ian very precisely. "So your cut is exactly two thousand nine hundred and fifty-seven pounds and twenty-six pence," he finished. "Here, I have got it all written down for you," he said and he handed Mike a piece of paper with all the figures on it. "Not bad, is it?"

"Not bad? I'll tell you what's not bad, the commission. If I could charge that much, I'd be a millionaire by now! Sorry Pippa, I know you don't make the rules, but it makes my blood boil. Ah, here are your drinks," said Mike as he nodded his thanks to the waiter.

"Well it's more than we had this time last week and we have had all the fun of the auction, but better still, Pippa and I met up, so altogether I think the commission was money very well spent," declared Ian stoutly.

"Bravo Uncle Ian, he's right, isn't he Marge?"

"Quite right Ian. Have a look at the menu, Mike and don't be so miserable. This is a celebration after all."

Mike looked rather crestfallen and Pippa felt quite sorry for him, so she changed the subject and asked Susie what she was studying at university.

Pippa couldn't have made a better choice of subject. Susie was in her second year of a Drama and Media Studies course and was very enthusiastic about it all. While they were chatting, Mike and Gaynor were poring over the menu and Ian just sat watching everyone with a warm glow of contentment. Pippa seemed to fit in seamlessly with everyone else and it confirmed his gut feeling yet again, that he and Pippa were meant for each other.

"Are you ready to order?"

A rather stern waitress had appeared beside them, notebook and pencil poised. These words brought Ian back from his reverie and he realised he had not even had a glimpse of the menu.

"Could I see the menu, Mike? Pippa have you chosen what you are having?"

"Not yet, I'll be quick though."

Mike was having none of it. He passed the menu to Ian and said, "Give us five minutes would you?" Which was more of a statement than a question and the waitress duly dismissed, sniffed and walked away to see if another group were better organised.

"Well, you know what I want, Dad," grinned Susie. She always had fish of some description if she was eating out and there was a long-standing family joke of her being a mermaid in another life, as she was also an expert swimmer.

"I'd forgotten about you and fish," said Ian, "but I was thinking of you last week when I did twenty-two lengths, not bad, eh?"

"Excellent. Next time I come home, we'll have a challenge. Actually I don't swim much in Exeter as the leisure centre is too far away from my flat, so I'm a bit rusty."

"Can we get back to the menu?" asked Mike wearily. "What would you like, Pippa?"

"It will have to be the onion soup, followed by the *Medallions de Porc*, I think."

"Same as me," smiled Gaynor.

"Well, I'm having the soup and the *Noix de Boeuf*. It sounds delicious." concluded Ian.

Mike, back in his comfort zone as project manager, beckoned the waitress to return and gave her their orders. The wine waiter was now hovering in the background and when she had finished writing, he asked Mike if he had selected a wine to go with the meal. As Mike prided himself on being a bit of a wine buff, this did not faze him one iota and he ordered a bottle of French Chardonnay and one of Fleurie, plus a bottle of sparkling water at Susie's request, and shortly after this, they were ushered into the dining room and over to a circular table for five by the window. It was attractively laid with a snowy white cloth and a bunch of spring flowers in the centre in a small silver vase.

They chose their seats and Pippa leaned back in her chair to look out of the window.

"Just look at those snowdrops!" she declared rapturously, and they all turned to share her gaze.

The grounds surrounding Le Vignot were more of a wild woodland than a neatly manicured garden. There was a luxurious carpet of snowdrops spreading between two very ancient oaks whilst, nestling against the boundary fences were masses of daffodils nodding to each other in the wind.

"Very pretty. It would make a marvellous backdrop for wedding photographs," joined in Gaynor with enthusiasm, and then not wanting anyone to take this the wrong way, added lamely, "I don't think they take wedding party bookings though."

Fortunately, at that point two waitresses arrived with their starters and at last they could concentrate on the food.

It was, as expected, absolutely delicious. The wine was just right, everyone was getting on well and Mike was beginning to mellow. By the time the desserts arrived, Gaynor was asking about Pippa's parents and he listened with interest. Ian had so far told them very little of Pippa's background which was not surprising, because amazingly, in their many and varied conversations, Ian and Pippa had never touched on this topic before, so he was listening intently, too.

"My parents are retired actually, and they live in the Lake District now, near to my Gran. She is nearly eighty six and finds she needs a great deal of help with getting about these days. They do a lot of hill walking too, when they can and weather permitting. We visited the Lakes several times a year when Tim and I were children, but I don't often have the opportunity now, which is a shame because I love it up there, despite the unpredictable weather," finished Pippa wistfully.

"We have been up to York, haven't we Gaye? But never as far north as Cumbria."

"It's well worth a visit, though it gets very overcrowded in the summer. You can't beat a day walking in the hills for recharging the batteries. Have you visited the Lakes, Ian?" Ian explained that despite working on projects in the north, he had never actually been to the Lakes either, then Mike in his usual impetuous fashion butted in,

"While we are on the subject of families, how about a bottle of bubbly to toast Mum and her precious jug?"

"What a nice idea. What do you think Ian? We could have a glass before we order the coffee," added Gaynor helpfully. Ian agreed so Mike called the waitress, who was hovering near the door to the kitchen, over to the table and asked her to pass on their request to the wine waiter, then he sat back and finished off the last of his Tiramisu.

"How is Jane getting on Gaye, I haven't seen her since Christmas?" enquired Ian, but before Gaynor had a chance to reply, Mike jumped up from the table, narrowly missing Pippa's glass of wine.

"What on earth's the matter Mike?" she asked, concerned.

"Sorry about that, but I've just remembered I said I'd take a picture of us all to send to Jane so she doesn't feel left out and I put the camera in my jacket pocket." His jacket was draped round the back of his chair and he fumbled about in all the pockets until he triumphantly produced his camera.

"Now then, if I stand with my back to the window, I should get a good shot of everybody. Yes," he said, squinting into the camera, "that's perfect... perhaps one from the other side too. Smile! Lovely. Do you think I should ask that waitress to take one of all of us?"

Gaynor patted his hand lovingly. She was thinking that in spite of his many gaffes, he was a really good father and Jane would appreciate the photos.

"Yes dear, why not?"

Mike called the waitress over again and explained what he wanted, then briefly told her how the camera worked and sat down with the others, giving them all tips as to how they should look at the camera to get the best picture.

Finally satisfied with the selection of shots, Mike retrieved his camera from the waitress who was by now Ian thought, looking decidedly miffed and sat down again. He scrolled through the pictures and, obviously pleased with himself, he declared, "That should do it, we've got some excellent ones here. I'll print them off later, so you can all have a look and email them to Jane as well. How on earth did we all manage without computers?"

"Well, I had a Polaroid if you remember Mike, but I have to admit digital cameras and computers are much more versatile," said Gaynor getting up from the table,

"I think I need to freshen up before the champagne arrives. Are you coming Pippa? Susie?" and the three ladies left the table, discussing the merits of cameras, computers and fluffy white cotton towels over paper ones.

"Do you know what Ian, I think I'll go too," said Mike. " Back in five," and Ian was left on his own, sipping the last dregs from his glass, a plan beginning to form in his mind.

Susie was the first to return.

"Oh good, you're on your own. I just wanted to tell you how much I like Pippa, and how attractive she is. We've had a really good talk," said Susie chattily.

"I'm glad you like her Susie. I quite like her myself," replied her uncle, with deliberate understatement.

"I don't suppose you have remembered that it is Valentine's Day on Tuesday?" Susie went on. "No, obviously not, typical man," she said chidingly, noticing Ian's face fall, then she added, "don't look so worried

Uncle Ian, there's still time to do something about it. Of course, I'm expecting loads!"

He laughed at her self-confidence, but he was also very grateful for the tip and told her so, only just in time before the others returned. They were closely followed by the waiter carrying the champagne in a bucket of ice, and five flutes. He uncorked the bottle, which to their amusement popped dramatically, then they waited quietly while he poured out the sparkling nectar and left them to it. Mike looked round the table to check they were all ready and then declared,

"To Mum, one of the best." and they all raised their glasses.

16

The party finally broke up at about half past four, with much hugging, kissing and many good-intentioned promises to meet up again soon.

Mike went off rather unsteadily, his arms around two of his favourite girls, with Gaynor telling him to mind her expensive suit – which Susie seemed to find hysterically funny, for some obscure reason.

Ian and Pippa got into his car and set off for Pippa's flat.

"What a wonderful afternoon Ian, I really like your family. Mike was all right, wasn't he?"

"Passable I suppose. He means well and his heart is in the right place. Anyway I am glad you enjoyed yourself."

"Susie is quite a character. Gaynor has her hands full with the pair of them, but she seems to thrive on it. What's Jane like?"

"Much quieter, probably more like her Mum, though she is just like Mike to look at."

"What a pity it's Monday tomorrow. I would love to have this weekend all over again," Pippa finished ruefully.

Ian thought this was quite the nicest thing anyone had ever said to him and told her so, adding,

"I hope we share lots more weekends, Pippa, starting this Friday."

"What? Have I got to wait until Friday?" she teased him.

He had not meant that at all and hastily invited her round for supper after work the next day. She was amused at his discomfort, but secretly loved his vulnerability, so she let him off lightly, saying as she got out of the car, "I was only joking. I could come round at about seven, will that be all right?"

"Just right. I'm looking forward to cooking for you," said Ian relieved and he blew her an extravagant kiss.

Ian had a lot to think about, but had decided that as soon as he got home, he would telephone Garth and see what he had arranged with Tim. No, blow that he thought impulsively, he could call round at Garth's house now instead, as it was on the way.

Fortunately Garth and Chrissie were at home, having tea with their twin boys, Matthew and Ben, who were squabbling amongst themselves as Ian rang the bell. Garth was delighted to see him and greeted him warmly at the door. They walked into the kitchen together and Ian accepted the cup of tea thrust at him then followed Garth into the lounge making sure he did not step on any of the bits of Lego that were strewn all over the carpet, fallout from the twins latest ruck. He sat down in a convenient chair, and launched straight into his reason for being there.

"I was on my way home from dropping Pippa off, so thought I would call and see how things were going with Tim."

"Obviously it all went well on Friday then," remarked Garth, with a quizzical look, his eyes dancing.

"Better than you might think – on both fronts," beamed Ian, "Mike and I could not believe how much money the jug made, and Pippa and I are definitely going somewhere." Then he added mysteriously,

"Watch this space."

Garth was really pleased to hear this and he got up, went over to the door and called to Chrissie, "Come in here, you have to hear this."

"What is it?" Chrissie asked, emerging from the kitchen. She was small and dark with a ponytail and lively brown eyes and looked much less than her 38 years, Ian noticed that she looked a little tired, but with two excitable five-year-olds in the house, this was not surprising.

"What have you two done now?" she asked quietly. Chrissie did most things quietly. She was calm and reflective, a perfect complement for the ebullient and positive Garth. He always told people fondly that she kept his feet on the ground, which must have been true because they had been happily married for over ten years.

"Ian has had a very successful few days and I thought you should hear it from the horse's mouth, especially as you gave him such good advice at the outset and lots of encouragement."

It did not take Ian long to explain about the auction and they were both surprised at how much was paid for the jug.

"And Pippa?" prompted Garth.

"Well, we went out Friday night, Saturday and today we had lunch with Mike and his family at Le Vignot. I am glad you gave me the confidence not to give up, Chrissie. You should definitely take up relationship counselling, you would make a fortune!"

Chrissie brushed this aside, saying, "I could see you were keen on Pippa and she would have been a fool not to see what a lovely man you are, so it wasn't difficult Ian. I am glad things are going well. Will we meet her soon?"

Ian did not have the opportunity to reply, as at this point thumps, yells and bangs were heard from upstairs and Chrissie went off quickly to see what mischief the twins were up to now.

"Those boys can be a handful," commented Garth affectionately, "but Chrissie is wonderful with them and now she is feeling so much better and they have started school, life is easier all round, but, back to Tim. Well, I haven't a lot to report really. We made contact and he is coming to meet me next week so that I can hear some of his tracks, then we will take it from there. He seems a nice enough chap so I hope we can do business."

"Thanks, Garth. I really appreciate your help. I will ask Pippa when she is free and we will arrange an evening out, just the four of us."

"It might be better if you come round here actually, as baby sitters are a bit of a problem at the moment."

Ian promised to give Garth a ring when he had spoken to Pippa, and after a lot of inconsequential chatter about nothing in particular, Ian finally made his excuses, called up the stairs to Chrissie to say he was leaving and headed for home to sort out his furniture, ready for the painters the next day.

17

Midnight found Ian sitting at his aged computer poring over lists of hotels in the Lake District. It had taken ages to boot up and he had let his mind wander back over the last few weeks while he waited. Unbelievable to think that this time last month he and Pippa had not met. Neither, at that stage, could he face moving on.

It had only been twelve days since she had called at his house to value the furniture. Some people might describe theirs as a whirlwind romance, but to him it felt as if they had known each other for ever.

He felt quite proud of the things he had achieved in such a short time and was comfortable with his more colourful life. It seemed to him that he had traded in his old life of mono for a new one of surround sound, and he was revelling in the full experience.

He had been to an auction and sold some of his emotional trappings.

He had kept his promise to Tim and now it was down to Garth.

The decorators would be arriving tomorrow, no, today to decorate the lounge and then it would be a new room. His room. All that was left now was to sort out his Valentine strategy. Having discovered that Pippa loved the Lakes, Ian's plan was to book a hotel for two nights at the weekend and invite her to have a romantic break with him there.

After reading about the pros and cons of several very smart hotels, Ian finally settled on the Killingbeck Ridge which boasted an outdoor swimming pool and a putting green. Not much use in February, he thought to himself, but it also claimed to be in a small village 'overlooking the lake and surrounded by majestic fells', which sounded suitably romantic, so he booked online for Friday and Saturday nights, printed out the booking confirmation sheet, then turned off the overheated computer and went to bed.

He awoke with a start to the sound of an engine cutting out close to his bedroom window. Due to his late-night session on the computer, he had overslept and suddenly realised it must be the painters arriving in their van. He was out of bed in a flash, and scrambling into some clothes, he dashed to the bathroom and splashed water on his face, then hurried downstairs in time to greet them.

Two men were unloading the van when he opened the door. Out came the dustsheets, a plastic box full of brushes, rollers, bottles of turps and several neatly folded cloths, followed swiftly by a pair of stepladders and two very large tins of paint.

The two men introduced themselves as they gathered up their equipment and walked into the house.

"Morning Mr Chisholm, Mike sent us over. I'm Rob and this is Dick. Which room will we be working in?"

They both wore very clean white overalls and had closely shaven heads – probably, Ian thought wickedly, making it easier for them to wash off any rogue splashes of paint.

"It's the front room. I moved all the furniture into the middle last night and I would be grateful if you could protect the carpet as much as possible, because I am not replacing it just yet."

"No problem." replied Rob, obviously the spokesman.

"We have brought lots of dustsheets, so we can cover everything." Putting the box down, he scanned the room.

"I will have to take the curtains down, though if that is all right."

"Of course. Sorry, I forgot about the window." apologised Ian.

"Green everywhere and white woodwork, is that it?"

Ian confirmed the colour scheme and left them to it.

There was no time for a run today; he had things to do in town, but first he had to shave and dress. When he was ready to leave, Ian thought he had better check on Rob and Dick. He could hear a lot of noise going on in the front room so he knocked loudly, then opened the door very gingerly in case one of them was working behind it.

The room had been transformed into a lunar landscape. It was completely swathed in large grey cloths and the shrouded furniture loomed eerily out of the dusty atmosphere.

"You two don't waste any time." he commented appreciatively. "I just wondered if you needed a drink before I go into town."

"No thanks, Mr Chisholm, we have brought our flasks. You get off, we'll be all right," replied Rob, his face now iced with a layer of white powder.

"Fine, I should be back in a couple of hours," said Ian and picking up his car keys from the hall table, he left the house.

18

Pippa dragged herself out of bed. Monday mornings were always difficult, especially after a really good weekend. She loved her job, but there was more to life than work.

Seeing the snowdrops and daffodils at Le Vignot had made her think of her Grandmother who had a garden full of them in her cottage at Hardale, near Grasmere. In fact, at this time of year, there would be daffodils in bud all over the Lake District. Perhaps she could persuade Ian to get up there sometime. She was sure he would love it.

She wondered if Ian knew it was Valentine's Day on Tuesday, probably not knowing him, but she had bought him a card anyway. In fact she had bought it when she was in London on the course – wishful thinking on her part, but amazingly, her wish had come true and she was positive he was the one for her. After all, at her age she reckoned she should know what she wanted.

She had decided to post her card at the main Post Office in Linchester to make sure it arrived on time, and as she got in her car to go to work, she wondered what Ian was cooking for her supper. It would make a nice change for someone else to cook, especially as she had a very busy day ahead. Seven o'clock couldn't come fast enough.

As it happened, Ian had chosen to make Spaghetti Bolognese followed by strawberries and ice cream for Pippa's supper and as there was nothing in his fridge, he had to call at the supermarket first, then he had to scour the town for a suitable Valentine's card. He had already decided not to post it, he would deliver it by hand very early on Tuesday morning, but finding a suitable one would be difficult. It had to strike the right note. Then there was the dilemma of the red roses. How many would be appropriate? Six, ten, twelve?

He gave himself a mental shake and told himself to do one job at a time. The easiest one was the supermarket and having done his shopping, he would tackle the others.

There weren't many shoppers about and he was up and down the aisles in next to no time. As he passed the card stand on the way to the checkout, he glanced along the racks, but could not find anything that appealed to him. It had been a forlorn hope, but worth a try.

Back in the car again, Ian registered that the weather was, for a change, quite bright and sunny, which he thought made a nice change and was very welcome as he had a lot of walking left to do. Having parked the car in town, he started his search for the perfect Valentine card. He did not want garish red hearts on a sparkly background, or two little bears blowing kisses to each other, neither did he want two figures walking along a windswept beach, nor one with a suggestive rhyme.

After the fourth shop he was beginning to panic, when he remembered a little art shop close to the Town Hall. From memory, he thought that along with artists' supplies of coloured pencils, charcoal, brushes, paints, sheets of cardboard, picture frames, large pieces of coloured paper and goodness knows what else, the shop also stocked a small selection of unusual handmade cards. Off he set again, feeling very hopeful, when his mobile phone rang. It was Mike.

"Just checking to see if Rob and Dick arrived on time, and don't shout down the phone, I have a terrible headache this morning."

"Too much champagne, I expect Mike," said Ian, smiling to himself. "Yes they turned up at about a quarter past eight. I am in town at the moment as I thought I would just leave them to it."

"Good. I thought Pippa fitted in very well yesterday. Did she enjoy the meal? Gaye and Susie are both taken with her. You had better hang on to this one Ian. Got to go now. Let me know if there are any problems," and with that the phone went dead.

Ian found Mike's attitude rather amusing. Typical of him to jump in with both feet and no mincing, but then he would not be Mike otherwise. He was delighted though, and relieved, that Pippa had evoked such a positive response in his nearest and dearest. It was just as well, because although their disapproval would have fazed him, his attraction to Pippa was so strong that he would never have given her up anyway.

He arrived at the art shop and went in, ducking to avoid hitting his head on a large wooden seagull which was suspended from the ceiling on a flexible wire. He asked the young man standing beside the till if the shop still stocked greetings cards and was directed to a section right at the back, beside a display of novelty mugs, where the riddle of the card was finally and satisfactorily solved when Ian discovered to his relief exactly what he had been looking for.

The card was of A5 size, printed on thick white paper with two stylised cut out hearts on the front and inside, the message was simple and to the point. It read 'Be My Valentine' in silver italic script. Perfect, he thought to himself and, delighted with his find, Ian made his way to the till, carefully avoiding a collision with the seagull on his way out.

Back into the sunshine once more, he just had the roses to buy, but the florist was right down the other end of town; Ian's marathon was not over yet. The lady in the flower shop was fortunately helpful and very patient and they eventually decided on ten red roses wrapped in cellophane, finished off with a red velvet bow. At last he had done everything and he could drive home for some well-earned lunch. As he drew nearer the house, Ian could see Mrs Ellison standing in her garden, brushing her path.

The bright sunshine had persuaded her to go outside and Ivy Ellison was now surveying the weeds that had appeared in her flower beds over the winter, leaning on her brush, wearing her favourite multicoloured patchwork jacket and a green felt hat with a floppy brim. She wondered for the umpteenth time if she was going to manage her garden again this year. It was all so much effort and expense and yet she disliked it looking a mess; she liked to see a colourful display when she opened her curtains in the morning, it suited her colourful nature. Equally, she hated to rely on other people for help. She concluded that getting older was no fun, but confusingly she still felt twenty-five inside and capable of anything in her head, it was just her eighty-year-old body that was letting her down.

Could she hear a car approaching? Ivy looked up from her neglected borders and realised it was Ian. She always had a little chat with him as she knew he missed his mother as much as she did. The way he had cared for her in her last few months had shown such selflessness and taken up so much of his time, that it was not surprising he had found it hard to come to terms with her not being there, but recently he seemed to be coming round. Probably, she thought wryly, due to that smart redhead he had been seeing. As he got out of the car, she called across to him, "It's gone awfully quiet in there Ian.

They have been making a terrible racket all morning. I expect they are having a lunch break now."

"Sorry about the noise, Mrs E. It is all the preparation they are doing. I expect you can hear the sander going," said Ian apologetically. "I'm sure when they start painting it won't be so bad. It's a nice day for a bit of gardening though."

"Yes, it is a welcome change from all that rain. Damp weather is no good for my old bones, it makes my fingers and knees ache."

"If you want a hand with the gardening, just let me know. I am not an expert, but I could manage with your supervision," he volunteered kindly.

"Give it another few weeks and I might just take you up on that, if my grandson doesn't come over. Who was that nice young lady I saw you with on Saturday? She's got lovely hair."

This amused Ian, he reckoned she must have an eye on the window the whole time.

"It was Pippa, she works at McFarlanes," he replied, then added provocatively, "she will be back again tonight as we are having supper together." What would she make of that, he wondered mischievously, then he went on, "I must go now Mrs E., I haven't had my lunch yet and I'm starving."

"Off you go love, it was nice to chat," said Ivy and with that, she limped slowly round to her back door dragging the brush behind her and thinking it was right what they said about love conquering all.

Rob and Dick were sitting in their van, eating sandwiches and reading newspapers, so Ian didn't disturb them. He unloaded the car and carried his shopping into the house. He had one last job to do before he made lunch. Walking into the kitchen, he took a large vase from the cupboard under the sink and filled it with water, then he placed the roses in it and carried them into the garage. He did not want Pippa seeing them tonight, as he wanted her to think he had forgotten all about Valentine's Day, it would make his surprise even more special.

The painters left at about four thirty and Ian went to see how much they had done. It was amazing what had been accomplished in one day. From what he could see, painting the walls was next, as they had already done the ceiling and all the undercoating. At this rate he guessed they would be done by Wednesday, and then he could add his finishing touches.

Preparing supper presented no problem for Ian as he enjoyed cooking and while he chopped the carrots and onions expertly, he was trying to picture Pippa's face when he gave her the roses. Secreted inside the bouquet – and this was his masterstroke – would be the computer printed hotel booking confirmation sheet. He hoped that the Grasmere area was the right choice. Well, he only had to wait one more day to find out.

As the sauce bubbled away He had time to write the card. Drinks at The Ship was his plan, replicating their first outing, then he would present her with the flowers. Ian mulled over the words he was going to use and having decided on his message, he opened the card and carefully wrote it down.

Pleased with his inventiveness, he put the card safely in its envelope, wrote her name in capitals on the front, and hid it in a drawer.

He was quite enjoying all this subterfuge and was really entering into the spirit of it, his sense of fun, though dormant for so long, had not expired completely.

The doorbell rang at ten minutes to seven, and Ian welcomed Pippa with the most enormous hug and kiss on the doorstep, hoping Mrs Ellison was keeping watch.

"Goodness, you only saw me yesterday, what is all this in aid of?" laughed Pippa straightening her jacket, then she added swiftly, "not that I am complaining, of course."

"Come inside and I'll explain," he murmured conspiratorially. When they were safely inside with the door shut, he put Pippa in the picture.

"Mrs Ellison next door is keeping tabs on me," he explained, "so, I thought I'd confirm her suspicions. Our friendship will be the talk of the church coffee morning now you know, I hope you don't mind, but it's only a bit of fun. She is very sweet, and was one of my Mum's best friends. I think she is a bit lonely now that Mum has gone. You see, after my father died, they saw a lot of each other as they were both widows then and she has known me since I was very small. Mrs E. has always been interested in what I am doing but recently, all of a sudden, she seems even more curious about my comings and goings."

Pippa listened patiently to his explanation, then declared generously with a chuckle, "No, of course I don't mind, especially if it means I am going to get an extra cuddle now and then."

She followed Ian into the kitchen and peered into the saucepans keeping warm on the hob.

"What have you been cooking? It smells wonderful and I am so-o-o hungry," she said and then she added, having realised what was on the menu,

"Mm, I love Spaghetti Bolognese. Have you got any Parmesan cheese?"

"Good, glad you approve and of course I have Parmesan cheese. Actually, on the subject of all things Italian, I wanted to ask you something. Go into the dining room and I will bring the food through."

The dining room, like the rest of the house, lacked the modern touch. The red velvet curtains were drawn against the February night and the floor was covered with a very busy Axminster in shades of red, yellow and grey. The oval wooden table was laid simply for two with an attractive cut glass bowl full of juicy strawberries right in the middle on a raffia mat. Against the wall adjoining the kitchen stood a matching sideboard on the top of which sat an Edwardian carved oak tantalus and along side it, in a plain wooden frame with a gilded edge, reclined a traditionally posed black and white photograph of a bride and groom, which Pippa presumed were Ian's parents.

She sat down at the table and wondered what on earth he was going to say to her, she had not got a clue what he might be planning.

A few minutes later, Ian approached the table with a steaming plate in either hand and he sat down opposite her, "Have you booked your holidays yet for this year?"

"No, I have been mulling over a trip to the States though," replied Pippa intrigued.

"Well I was wondering if you would like to come to Italy with me at Easter. I have been investigating possible places to visit and I think Florence would be good, especially as it has a museum containing excellent examples of ceramics amongst other things and it is not far from Pisa. I have always wanted to see the Leaning Tower."

He looked at Pippa who had gone very quiet, which made him a little unnerved.

"Well, say something, you are making me nervous," he said.

"I was just thinking how much you have changed, and not in a bad way. You are full of surprises, and I love it. It sounds like a splendid idea. I have never been to Italy and I would really like to go with you. I will have to check with work, but in principle, yes, yes and yes," she replied emphatically, cheeks glowing.

It was the preferred option after all. He had done it. Ian silently applauded his own brazen attitude. The boring man had been well and truly laid to rest and he felt himself to be a very lucky man instead. His Valentine surprise would top it all off nicely.

"Good, that is the right answer," he said boldly and smiling secretly to himself, asked, "Now, where did I put that Parmesan?"

19

It was still dark when Ian's alarm broke into his dreams. He woke up slowly, savouring memories of last night's supper with Pippa.

The evening had been a great success, and not just the cooking. They had discussed Italy over the meal and afterwards as they had washed up together. Then they had pored over the books he had borrowed from the library and had looked on the internet too, where he had shown her all the information he had found. Pippa had added some suggestions of her own and she had promised to ask Alice if she knew of any good deals on cheap flights and to speak to James McFarlane about having some time off over Easter so they could get on and arrange the trip.

The alarm reminded him again that it was time to be up, and this time he switched it off and got up. If he didn't make a move now, he wouldn't have time to deliver the card and be back before Rob and Dick arrived.

He jogged down the road in a light drizzle of rain. The streets were deserted except for a milk float humming and clinking on its rounds and an eager paperboy on his bike, bag flapping behind him.

Pippa's block of flats was in darkness as he approached, so he was confident she was not up yet. He slowed to a walk and on arriving at the entrance doors, searched for her letterbox. Having found it, he retrieved the precious missive from his inside pocket, lifted the flap and posted it. Ian felt his face breaking into a grin at the thought of how surprised she would be when she looked for her post and found the card. He felt sure she had not got a clue that he had remembered what day it was.

By the time he arrived back home, the sun was rising. Everywhere looked damp and the air was redolent of moist earth and sodden leaves, but the persistent drizzle had abated. If it held off, he had made up his mind to start on the garage which was well overdue for a clear-out. That, he reckoned, should keep him busy for most of the day as he was anticipating several trips to the dump, but first he would need a good breakfast and he set about sorting this out.

He was just finishing his toast, when Rob and Dick duly turned up and shortly afterwards the doorbell rang for a second time. When Ian opened the door, he found Mike standing there, looking very pleased with himself.

"Morning Mike."

"I have got something for you, I hope you like it," he started without preamble, as he handed Ian a small brown envelope. Ian took the envelope from his outstretched hand, and Mike went on, "While I'm here I thought I could see how things are progressing. I was hoping the lads would be finished tomorrow as I have another small job for them to do this week."

Ian opened the envelope while he was talking.

"Thanks. What on earth ..." he began. Mike was looking very smug and Ian, realising he was looking at Mike's latest Patrick Lichfield efforts, went on, "These are very good, especially this one of Pippa, Susie and me."

"I knew you would like that one. I'm thinking of taking up photography actually. I might do a course at the college while Gaye is at yoga. I will have to check it out on the college website."

Ian knew Mike liked to keep busy, and the photos were very good, so he said encouragingly, "Why not?

These photos are excellent. Perhaps you could join the local camera club too. They are always having exhibitions in the Town Hall. Talking of photographs, I have found some in an old leather suitcase upstairs that I want you to have a look at. I don't recognise any of the people in them, but I thought you might."

"Right, I will have a look, but not today, I've got too much to do already."

"OK, I will be in the garage if you need me." Mike acknowledged this with a nod of the head, and opened the sitting room door to calls of, "Morning Boss" and, "Checking up on us are you?"

Ian headed off in the opposite direction and outside to the garage. He pulled open the heavy doors and took stock of the task he had set himself. Where should he start?

Since his father's death some twenty years before, Ian and his mother had not had a lot to do with the garage. It was a repository for dusty boxes full of this and that and some rusty tools, plus anything they had replaced with a more up-to-date version and not thrown away. There was also a corner where Ian kept a few bottles of wine that he had no room for in the house.

Norman Chisholm had been an amateur engineer-cum-handyman and member of the local model steam railway society which was a perfect foil for his day job as a clerk at the County Council, and it was his father's enthusiasm for all things mechanical that had set Ian off on his engineering career. He knew he would have his work cut out investigating the contents of all the old biscuit tins and cardboard boxes that were piled high everywhere. He took a deep breath and opened the first one.

Mike had finished talking to Rob and Dick and being very happy with their progress walked round to the garage to let Ian know he was going. He did not see him straight away, but noticing a pile of rusty paint tins and dilapidated tools just outside the door Mike called out loudly, "Are you in there, Ian?" and, on hearing an affirmative grunt, went on, "They are getting on very well with the painting; on schedule for finishing tomorrow. Sorry I can't stay and help with the clearing out, but I have several people to see this morning and a couple of estimates to do. I shouldn't think there is anything worth salvaging in there," he finished, turning over an old canvas bag distastefully with the tip of his foot.

"No, it's mostly rubbish so far," called Ian from the darkest recesses of the garage, and straightened his back to look at Mike.

"It doesn't matter, I've started, so I'll finish," he added light-heartedly.

"Right. How are you getting on with Pippa?"

"Fine, thanks." Then Ian's eyes alighted on something he had not seen for a very long time, and he pulled it out from underneath his old bicycle, which was lying in a twisted heap on the floor, inner tubes protruding from two very flat tyres which were still clinging on to the rather rusty rims.

"Hey, Mike, do you remember this?" Ian held aloft a go-cart made from a stained piece of charred wood and some battered pram wheels, for Mike to see.

"Well, I never, Old Smokey!" cried Mike. "Those were the days. Why did we call it that, do you remember?"

"Because Dad rescued the wood from the bonfire at a derelict house," replied Ian straight away.

"The fuss Mum made when he came home covered in ash," he went on thoughtfully. Mike nodded his head and Ian thought he looked a trifle sad.

"Chuck it out," he said gruffly, "we are not ten years old any more. Must dash," and he was off down the drive and into his 4x4.

Ian carried the go-cart outside and dumping it on the 'unwanted' pile of junk beside the boot of his car, thought to himself that there were times when he just could not fathom Mike at all. Who would have thought their Old Smokey would have choked him up like that? Nice to know that he could feel sentimental sometimes though, and he went back to see what other ancient curios he could unearth.

Two miles away in her flat, Pippa was getting herself up and dressed. She hoped against hope that there would be a card for her from Ian, but the letterbox was downstairs in the hall and she could not, or would not, go downstairs in her silk pyjamas.

Bucking the current trend, the post was delivered to her flat before eight thirty most mornings, so she would know straight away if she had been lucky or not. Feeling a bit foolish at her age to set such store by a Valentine's card, and with her heart beating faster, she opened the box.

The post had arrived and there was some junk mail in the box plus two brown envelopes, but there at the bottom, underneath everything else, was one medium-sized white one. Her hands trembled as she undid the envelope and took out the carefully chosen card. Very slowly she opened it. Inside there was a printed Valentine message and underneath that in capital letters, were the words:

DO NOT MISS THE BOAT
MEET ME AT THE SHIP AT EIGHT!

She read the message, then laughed out loud and looking round her sheepishly, thought it was a good job there was no one else in the lobby or they would think she was completely mad. She looked at the envelope again and saw that there was no stamp on it and realised with a warm glow that Ian must have got up at the crack of dawn just to deliver the card. He had not failed her, the man was a star.

20

It was late afternoon, and after rather more trips to and from the dump than he had anticipated, when a very grubby and slightly weary Ian called it a day in the garage. He had cleared the floor and sorted through numerous boxes and tins, finding very little worth keeping. He had thrown away half full tins of paint, bristle-less brushes and broken toasters, plus goodness knows how many old tobacco tins filled with useless nuts and bolts.

The old bikes had been discarded, along with a few very flat footballs and heaps of leaves that had blown underneath the garage doors over the years and piled up against the rough brick walls.

Ian felt the satisfaction of a job well done and had decided to put up some new shelves in due course, to serve as a more practical wine cellar.

Who knows, he thought to himself as he walked in through the back door and wiped his feet, he might even use the garage as a garage now especially if, as he had been considering, he decided to change his car for something a bit more classy. Yet more to contemplate and, along with all his other plans, he reckoned he had quite a lot to look forward to in the foreseeable future.

Rob and Dick were just packing up to leave, so he had a quick word with them then treated himself to a glass of cold beer and went to view his transformed sitting room.

The walls and ceiling were painted the very pale shade of green he had chosen and there was only a small amount of glossing left to do, so they would definitely be finished midmorning the next day, meaning Ian could easily get the room back in action by Friday, just before he left for his weekend away with Pippa, perhaps even sooner than that with a bit of luck.

He closed the door and noticed for the first time that there was some post lying on the floor in the hall, behind the front door. There was a large red envelope, several items of advertising and a postcard from Garth. Why was it he wondered, not for the first time, that postcards sent from abroad always took so long to turn up, inevitably arriving long after your friends had returned safely home?

After looking at the snowy scene on the front of the card and quickly reading Garth's cheery message, Ian looked at the envelope. He did not recognise the handwriting and it was not his birthday. What could it be? After a day in the depths of the garage, Valentine's greetings were the last thing on Ian's mind. He opened it up and a large red heart flashed into his line of vision. He realised instantly that this was a Valentine's card from Pippa. She had written under the caption 'I Give You My Heart Valentine', 'Better late than never', followed by a big red question mark.

Ian was very touched and diverted by her card and the message she had written, thinking yet again how much better his life had been since they had met and he hoped Pippa had liked the one he had sent her just as much. He gave the card pride of place on his kitchen window sill, finished his beer and went upstairs to have a shower and wash the cobwebs out of his hair.

Pippa arrived home from work with much the same idea in mind, but first she needed something to eat. She raided her freezer and selected a shepherd's pie and vegetables which she put in the microwave straight away.

Ian's card was displayed on the mantelpiece in her sitting room, and while she was waiting for her meal to be ready, she read it again, a smile playing round the corners of her mouth. Her day dreaming was disturbed by her mobile and when she picked it up, she saw from the display that Tim was calling her.

"Hello Pip, you wanted me to let you know how I got on with Garth," he started, "well, he was quite complimentary about the CD we prepared for him, but he wants to have another meeting when he has discussed matters with his partner because he felt the quality of the recording was not as good as it might be."

"That's a shame, does it mean he is not interested?"

"Not at all, he suggested we perform again in his studio to get a more professional sound."

"Superb!" she exclaimed, "I expect you are all over the moon."

"I haven't told the others yet, but we are having a band practice tonight, so I will let them know then. This is all Ian's doing, and I'm really grateful, so you will let him know, won't you?"

"Of course I will, I'll tell him when I see him later," said Pippa feeling pleased for her brother, who deserved a break after his years of hard work. At that point, the microwave pinged insistently at her.

"I will have to go now," she told Tim. "My supper is ready. Can you hear the microwave beeping at me? I will have a proper chat with you tomorrow."

"Right, speak to you then," and with that Pippa went off to enjoy her meal, reminding herself that she had better be quick if she didn't want to be late for her Valentine rendezvous with Ian.

21

Ian was sitting in The Ship, waiting for Pippa. He was eager to see her, but a bit anxious too. He had the flowers concealed under his coat beside him on the seat with their secret message safely hidden between the blooms, but he was still not quite sure if he had pitched it right. Only time would tell. He hoped she would arrive soon as the suspense was beginning to get to him.

Unlike their last visit, The Ship was quite busy this evening and he had been very lucky to find somewhere to sit down. He tugged at his shirt nervously and took another sip of his beer. Where was she? The door was obscured by small groups of young people chatting and laughing together, so when Pippa walked in, he did not see her at first.

Pippa noticed him straight away though, and walked right over, her eyes shining and her glorious red hair in a thick plait resting on her shoulder. Ian thought she looked more beautiful than ever, and said so.

"Thank you kindly," she said demurely as she sat down beside him.

"I got your card Ian," then she added audaciously, with a twinkle in her eye, "at least I think it was from you. Seriously though Ian, thank you for that too," and she gave him a brief kiss on the lips.

"Actually, I had a card as well, but I can't imagine who from," he joined in playfully.

"Only one?" she retorted with a laugh.

"Yes, but then there was only one person I wanted one from," he said gallantly, then he added, "I have something else for you here," and he brought out the roses from underneath his coat, with a dramatic flourish.

"Oh Ian, they are lovely." Pippa gasped, astonished and delighted with his gesture. She had never expected flowers as well as a card. The cellophane crackled as she gathered the roses nearer to take in their scent, then Pippa suddenly noticed a piece of paper folded inside them. Ian was watching her closely.

"What is this?" she asked, looking at him whilst extricating the paper from its hiding place. Ian did not reply, but had the strangest feeling that time was standing still and that they were the only two people left in the pub. She read the sheet of paper quickly and then he noticed a tear creeping down Pippa's cheek and he was immediately transported back to the hubbub in the bar.

"Are you all right Pippa? What's wrong?" He asked, alarmed.

She had in fact been overwhelmed by his romantic gesture; it was such a leap of faith for him and he had come such a long way emotionally in the last few weeks that she fully appreciated all the effort he must have put in to achieve his Valentine surprise. Slowly, Pippa wiped away her tears and smiled at him mistily. Clutching the piece of paper in her hand and clearing her throat, she finally found her voice.

"I'm fine, but this is so unexpected Ian, I just do not know what to say."

Now Ian was seriously worried. He knew it was too much, too soon. Falling back into old habits, he started to apologise, but she cut him off short saying fiercely, "Don't you dare apologise, Ian Chisholm! What you have done is so thoughtful, so romantic, so lovely, so you. It is just such a wonderful surprise. What made you think of it? I can't imagine a better way to spend the weekend and I am sure I can slip away early on Friday afternoon so that we can avoid the worst of the traffic. Thank you so, so much," she finished breathlessly.

Ian squeezed her hand. The relief was immense and his heart was full of love for her.

"I'm so happy Pippa, I was really scared for a moment that I had misjudged the situation. Let me get you a drink and I'll tell you all about the hotel," he said, happily.

"You are sweet, Ian. But surely you must know by now how much I like spending time with you? I am very thirsty though, so I think I will have a lemonade please, with plenty of ice."

"Right. I'll try not to be too long," he said and went off to the bar to fetch her drink.

He was back in next to no time with the lemonade and another beer for him, plus two packets of peanuts for good measure.

"Now then, back to the hotel," he said briskly. "I picked the Killingbeck Ridge because it seemed to be in a very romantic setting. It boasts an outdoor swimming pool, you know, but I'm not so sure about that at this time of year."

"Actually, I know the place you are talking about," said Pippa. " It is just outside the village where my Gran lives. How is that for a coincidence?"

"Well, it was obviously meant to be then," said Ian revelling in his good fortune at picking such an appropriate place for their weekend away.

Pippa took a long drink of her lemonade, then replied, "It is in quite a picturesque setting and I have often wondered what it is like inside there. You will love it," she said exuberantly. "Roll on Friday; I must ring Mum and Dad to tell them we are coming," she finished, flushed with excitement.

"I'm looking forward to meeting them all," said Ian still pleased with himself for having chosen so well and delighted by Pippa's unfeigned enthusiasm for the whole enterprise.

They left the pub in high spirits, Pippa clutching the roses tightly and before they parted company, Ian invited her round to his house the next evening to see the results of the 'makeover'.

"I can't wait, I bet it looks good. Oh dear, I almost forgot to give you a message from Tim. With all your surprises you put it out of my head. Garth has heard the CD and he wants to make another recording in his studio to get a better result."

"That sounds promising. We will have to keep our fingers crossed for him."

"By the way," he added, just as she was unlocking her car, "I found that old frame I was telling you about. It cleaned up rather well. Remind me to show you tomorrow evening."

"I will try, but I have got quite a bit on my mind at the moment, as you well know," she joked, "are you sure you don't want a lift?"

"No, I'm fine, thanks all the same. I am really enjoying my running. I had forgotten how good it feels to get the heart pumping!"

"I'll leave you to it then and go and ring my parents. They are going to be so surprised," she said and with that she started her car.

The engine purred into life and snatching a kiss through the car window, Ian set off to jog home, revelling in that warm feeling that comes with a job well done.

22

Rob and Dick arrived, as usual the next morning and the painting was all finished ahead of schedule, by eleven o'clock.

"Just give it a couple of hours and you can put everything back in place," advised Rob, wiping his brush on an old piece of cloth. Dick was busy packing up all their gear and, before he knew it, Ian was alone in the house once more.

While he was waiting for the paint to harden, he decided to spend his time sorting out that old suitcase from the spare room. He thought one of the photos might look good in the old silver frame, but first he planned to have an early lunch.

He emptied a tin of vegetable soup into the smallest of his saucepans and then went upstairs to fetch the suitcase while it was warming through.

With the suitcase conveniently settled on the dining room table, the soup poured into a bowl and some crusty bread to hand, he was ready to start, but then the doorbell rang and he had to put his plans on hold.

He was surprised to see that it was his brother. Ian had not expected Mike to return so soon having only just been round the day before. Mike was dressed for the weather with a Linchester Wanderers bobble hat pulled down over his ears, a thick check shirt, cable-knit sweater and charcoal grey body warmer, some black cord trousers and his site boots.

"I had half an hour, so I thought I would come and look through those photographs you were talking about," said Mike in a businesslike fashion, removing his hat and stuffing it in the pocket of his trousers.

"Great minds think alike," quoted Ian, "I brought the case down from upstairs five minutes ago, so that I can have a proper look through while I eat my lunch. Come in, I am just having a bowl of soup. Do you want some?"

"Yes please," replied Mike eagerly, rubbing his hands together and kicking off his boots in the hall.

"It's a bit parky out there."

He marched through into the warm kitchen in his socks and left Ian to shut the front door behind him.

"Mmm, vegetable, my favourite," he commented approvingly, "I'll sort myself out," he said, selecting a bowl from the kitchen cupboard. "Where is the case?"

"It is on the dining room table. Come and have a look."

Mike carried his hot soup and bread into the dining room with Ian close behind him and together they examined the suitcase.

He dismissed all the cards after a cursory glance through them.

"Well, you can throw all that lot away. Now we're down to the interesting bit."

There must have been about twenty photographs, most of them groups of people in all manner of poses, carefully arranged for the camera. Some of them were a bit creased, but overall they were not in bad condition.

Mike looked at each of the photographs in turn, in between mouthfuls of bread and soup, saying nothing while Ian peered over his shoulder and waited for the verdict.

"I think I need my glasses on for this job, hang on a minute."

Mike took a small black leather case from the pocket of his body warmer, which he had taken off and placed on an empty chair, out of which came a pair of rimless glasses. They were soon fitted neatly on the bridge of his nose and he re-examined the photograph he was holding in his hand.

"What do you think, then?" asked Ian, unable to contain himself any longer. He was becoming more and more curious by the minute.

"I think some of these are Dad's relations, judging by the noses," said Mike flippantly, "but I can't make out this one."

He was staring at a photo of two couples, one in their twenties and the other a bit older, seated on a rug in the countryside, obviously sharing a picnic.

"That one is Mum," he said pointing to a youngish woman in a flowery summer frock, "and the bloke next to her is Dad, but who the other two are, beats me. I am afraid that is the best I can do."

Ian felt a bit disappointed, but it had, after all, been a long shot.

"Well thanks for trying, Mike. I suppose now this picture will remain a mystery for ever. When you have finished your lunch, would you come and help me put some of the furniture back in the front room? The paint should be dry by now."

Mike looked at his watch, which Ian couldn't help noticing was a new Tag Heuer. Business must be good, he thought and presumed Mike had finally sold the last two of six houses he was building right next to the golf course. He remembered Mike complaining a few weeks before that a subcontractor had let him down and the houses would be finished later than he had planned. It would seem that they had made up for lost time, and he said, “That’s a smart watch. Have you finally sold those two houses?”

“Yes,” said Mike, letting him have a better look at his new watch, but not meeting his eye and then adding, a little too quickly, Ian thought, “now I am starting on the church hall redevelopment. Right,” he went on, getting up from the table, “I will have time to help you, but I can’t be long because I have to fit in a site meeting before the match tonight. After all, it is the least I can do after you giving me that soup. Let’s go.”

The thought crossed Ian’s mind that Mike was up to something, but it was no sooner thought, than it went out of his head, when he heard Mike summoning him with, “Come on, Ian. I haven’t got all day.”

23

By the time Pippa turned up that evening, Ian had fitted the blinds, hoovered the carpet, unrolled the rug and had it strategically placed under his coffee table, then he had arranged the new cushions on his chairs as artistically as possible.

He had brought the silver frame down to show her and, looking at it again he was quite impressed at the way it had cleaned up. It was an art nouveau style frame with leaves curling round the rim, then joining up at the top right hand corner with a tulip like flower. He felt sure she would like it, but if he was wrong, he was happy to keep it himself and find a suitable corner for it somewhere. Unfortunately, he had still not sourced an appropriate picture to grace the frame. It was a shame, because he felt sure it would look so much more interesting with something in the middle of it instead of just an ugly empty space. Just then, an idea occurred to him which he thought might just work.

Now, where had he put those pictures Mike had taken at Le Vignot? He searched around in the kitchen, looked in the sideboard drawers in the dining room and then remembered he had taken the envelope upstairs and left it in his room.

Having finally successfully located the envelope exactly where he thought it might be, Ian extricated the snap of him with Susie and Pippa and he tried it in the frame. As he had hoped, it was a perfect fit. He was just wiping his finger marks off the polished frame, when Pippa arrived.

"Hello again," she said happily, giving him a kiss on both cheeks, "what are you hiding behind your back?"

Ian revealed the frame, now complete with photograph, and handed it to her.

"This is amazing," cried Pippa in delight. "I love it, and I love the picture too. Is this one of the photos Mike took on Sunday?"

"I think it is the best one, actually. I am glad you like the frame. Is it good enough for your collection?"

"Of course it is. Are you prepared to part with it though? It really is a delightful frame," she said admiringly.

"I would like you to have it, it will look good with all your others and I hope it will remind you of a very happy afternoon," he said with a grin.

"You really are a darling Ian, in that case, thank you very much. Now, let's have a look at the transformation!"

Without wasting another moment, Ian threw open the sitting room door and stood back for her to go in first.

"Wow, doesn't it look good," she said, suitably impressed. "I thought the cushions would finish it off and you were quite right about those blinds too, now it is my turn. Wait there," she said mysteriously and to his surprise she went back out of the front door. She returned moments later carrying a large plant in an earthenware planter. It had very healthy looking glossy green leaves which made it difficult for her to see where she was going but with a bit of help from Ian, she eased it through the door without too much trouble.

"This is to christen your new room, Ian. I left it outside the front door when I arrived because I wanted to give you a surprise for a change," she said gleefully.

"Pippa, you are priceless," said Ian, pleased with her gift and equally charmed by her thoughtfulness, then he added fondly, "in fact you are a little gem. Thanks, I hadn't thought of a plant myself, but you are quite right, it is just what the room needs. Shall we put it over by the window?" They settled on an appropriate place for the plant together and then Pippa asked him,

"As you have done this room so well, what will you start on next, I wonder. What about the dining room?"

"Oh, please! I have run out of ideas and energy for the moment," laughed Ian.

"Let's go and make a cup of coffee then, and I will tell you what my parents said," suggested Pippa kindly.

"Are they looking forward to seeing you?" Ian asked as they walked through to the kitchen.

"Yes they are," she replied. "They were really surprised when I told them we were coming and so was Gran when I spoke to her, but they can't wait to meet you."

"What on earth have you told them about me?" asked Ian, slightly alarmed.

"Oh, only that you are tall, dark and handsome, very intelligent and a millionaire," she teased him.

The dining room door was open as they passed, and Pippa noticing the old leather case on the table and the photographs laid out across the top in haphazard piles, said,

"More photographs, Ian. Can I take a look?"

"Of course you can," he said, slightly preoccupied with his selection of two suitable mugs from a selection on the kitchen worktop. "Go and have a look and I will bring the coffee through in a minute."

"Who are all these people?" asked Pippa, when he joined her not long afterwards.

"I haven't a clue," replied Ian carelessly, putting a mug of coffee down on the table beside her and standing at her shoulder.

"Mike doesn't know either, though we think they might be some of my father's family," he said. Then he picked up the photograph of the picnic party to show her.

"He pointed out that this one has Mum and Dad in it, plus a mystery couple."

Pippa took the photograph from his hand and examined it very carefully for a minute or two.

"The mystery couple seem a bit familiar, but I can't quite place them," she said, perplexed.

"Now I look at it again, I can't see how I did not recognise my parents myself, especially when you compare it with this one," he went on, pointing to the wedding photograph she had noticed that evening she liked to remember as their Italian evening.

At that point, Pippa gave a little squeak of excitement – she had experienced a Eureka moment.

"I think I know who they are, Ian," she gasped.

"Well, tell me, for Heaven's sake," he begged.

"I have a hunch ... they are James McFarlane and his wife Hannah. Obviously when they were much younger," responded Pippa slowly.

"Really? Are you sure?" Asked a somewhat startled Ian. Pippa's revelation was completely unexpected and he had to consciously close his mouth which he suddenly realised had fallen open in amazement.

"Almost ninety-nine point nine per cent. When you mentioned your parents' wedding photograph, something clicked. You see, James invites all the staff round to his house for drinks at Christmas every year – he calls it his Seasonal Wassail. Anyway, they have a piano in the sitting room and on the top of it are several photographs of James and Hannah when they were younger."

"I do not believe it! What a coincidence. I wonder how they knew each other?" Ian asked, still somewhat stupefied.

"I haven't a clue, but I know how I can find out," she said helpfully. "If you agree, I will take the photo into work tomorrow and ask James if we are right and if so, how they all became friends."

"Of course, what a good idea," agreed Ian.

"I will put it in my handbag right now so I don't forget it. With a bit of luck all will be revealed tomorrow morning." And with that, Pippa went into the hall in search of her bag, leaving Ian to contemplate that truth was quite often much stranger than fiction and how his decision to clear out the house and sell his mother's china had led him on a journey of many twists and turns.

Surely now he could settle down and look forward to the weekend away without being ambushed by another unexpected event? But fate had decreed otherwise, as Ian was about to find out.

24

Pippa was as good as her word and first thing on Thursday morning, she went to talk to James. He was in his office, sitting at his rather grand leather-topped antique partners' desk with the door open, checking the accounts for last week's auction and looking very pleased with himself.

"Come in Pippa," he said affably when he saw her approaching his door, "what can I do for you?"

"I would like you to solve a mystery actually."

"Intriguing. If I can, I will. Fire away."

Pippa produced the photograph and passed it over the desk and into the hand he offered her.

"What can you tell me about this picture?"

James studied the photograph and looked up at Pippa, a perplexed expression on his face.

"Where on earth did you get this?" he asked mystified.

Pippa gave him a brief potted history of the picture and was relieved to see a smile spread across his face.

"Well, I am happy to solve your mystery for you. This photograph was taken more years ago than I care to remember. It is of Hannah and I having a day out, with Norman and Vera Chisholm. But you suspected as much, didn't you, or you wouldn't be showing me the photograph now? Norman and I were both keen members of the Linchester model steam railway society and though he was somewhat older than I was, we got on really well. That picture was taken on the annual picnic, I seem to remember we were in Hampshire, near the Watercress Line, I think.

As a young auctioneer, Vera was always picking my brains as to the value of her latest discovery, and asking me about what to look for on her forays into the junk shops and jumble sales. Later, of course I expect she frequented the charity shops that have sprung up all over the place. They sometimes have rich pickings I believe. Strangely enough, as far as I know, she never bought anything from an auction. She told me they were too intimidating for her. They were a lovely couple, but we lost touch after Hannah and I moved away from Linchester for a few years, shortly after that picture was taken."

Pippa was bursting to tell him about Vera's jug and when his reminiscences ended, she finally had her chance.

"There is a nice twist to the end of this story, James. You know I said it was a photograph of my boyfriend's parents? Well, he put some of his mother's furniture in our last auction, along with several bits and pieces of china. That was how we met. In particular, there was one rather nice Clarice Cliff jug," she finished elatedly, eyes shining, waiting to see what his reaction would be.

"Well I never!" he exclaimed. "I don't believe it. So that was Vera's jug? Gracious me. Just goes to show, I must have taught her something then," and he gave a hoot of laughter.

He was still chortling to himself and shaking his head in surprise, as Pippa left the room on her way to telephone Ian and tell him what she had discovered.

Their conversation was destined to be a brief one as some clients had arrived while she had been talking to James and they were waiting for her in the auction hall.

Ian had been expecting her to phone him and he answered her call straight away.

"I was right, Ian," she began before he had time to say 'hello' then she went on, "it was James and Hannah. They were all on a picnic with the model steam railway society."

"Well, that explains it then, clever girl! Now I will be able to tell Mike that the mystery is solved. Actually I am just off to see him about the weekend. Wish me luck."

"You don't need any luck, he will be fine," answered Pippa bracingly.

"I thought you might bring your weekend bag round tonight, so I can pack the car for our trip," said Ian.

"Good idea, I will, then you can pick me up straight from work tomorrow, which will give us an extra half an hour," said Pippa eagerly. At that moment, Beth put her head round the door and beckoned to Pippa urgently, so she ended her conversation with Ian rather abruptly and said,

"I have to go now, Ian, clients waiting," and then she rung off.

Ian summarily dismissed, left the house as soon as he had finished talking with Pippa and arrived at Mike's house to find Gaynor in the drive, about to get out of her car with a bag full of shopping.

"Hello, Ian, have you come to see Mike?" she asked, "He is probably in the office. He has been in there a lot over the last few days and is being very secretive, making mysterious telephone calls with the door closed. I think he is probably cooking up some deal or other now all those houses are sold, but he hasn't told me anything, as usual."

"I wanted to talk to both of you, as a matter of fact," said Ian, smiling at her.

"That sounds ominous," and she smiled back while she brandished her keys at the lock. "Come in then."

Gaynor ushered Ian into the hall and Mike, on hearing voices, came out to meet them.

"Hello, you two," he said, looking faintly surprised.

"Hello dear. Ian has got some news for us, but I just want to put this meat in the fridge first, I will join you both in a minute," and with that Gaynor walked off towards the kitchen.

"What can I do for you this fine morning Ian? Come in, come in."

Ian followed Mike into his office, and being aware of a big difference in the state of the room, commented, "It is amazingly tidy in here, I can even see the chairs and daylight through the windows!"

"Yes, Gaynor had one of her 'white tornado' moments while we were at the auction. She has made such a good job of it, now I can't find anything," grumbled Mike good naturedly.

"I have identified the mystery couple," said Ian, sitting himself down on one of Mike's black leather swivel chairs.

"And?" asked Mike, pouring him a cup of coffee from the flask Gaynor made fresh for him each morning, then settling himself at his desk with his back to the computer.

"Thanks, Mike. Well, they are James and Hannah McFarlane."

"Who might they be?" asked Mike quizzically.

"The auctioneer who sold Mum's jug and his wife," declared Ian jubilantly.

Gaynor joined them in the office at that point and Mike repeated Ian's news.

"Really? What a coincidence. How on earth did they know each other?"

"Yes, and how did you work that out?" added Mike, with a look of enquiry on his face.

Ian explained Pippa's detective work and they all agreed how strange it was that the jug his mother had bought all those years ago had been the catalyst in bringing them all together. Then Ian, unable to put it off any longer, took a deep breath and went on,

"I have something else to tell you both. I am going away for the weekend, so I won't be coming for Sunday lunch this week. I am off to the Lakes with Pippa," he finished very quickly and rather sheepishly.

Mike opened his eyes wide, but said nothing. It was Gaynor who spoke first.

"What a lovely idea Ian, she was telling us at Le Vignot how much she liked it up there."

After a slight pause Mike said thoughtfully, "You two are seeing a lot of each other."

"Why not?" asked Gaynor quickly, hoping Mike was not going to pour cold water on the idea, "they are both grown-ups, after all."

"So they are. Well, if you want my opinion, I think you are a very lucky man. I like Pippa and she obviously likes you, so what more do you want?"

"Thanks Mike, I'm really looking forward to it," said Ian feeling as if a weight had been lifted from his shoulders. Still finding it a bit hard to discuss personal matters with his brother, he tried a more practical line.

"It will probably be a five-hour drive to get there, but as long as it doesn't snow, it should be all right. It is a good thing that I have just had my car serviced," then keen to be off and away he added, "Well now I have brought you both up to speed, I will have to get back to the house and pack my bag. See you when I get home."

He finished his coffee and got up to leave, when quite unexpectedly, Mike walked round the desk and gave him a big hug, saying rather emotionally,

"I have a good feeling about all of this, it could be the start of something really special. Have a good time, mate."

Gaynor also added her good wishes plus, just for good measure, another hug and Ian went on his way thinking, fondly, that Pippa had been right all along and that Mike was mellowing in his old age.

There was one more call he had to make before he went home to start his packing. He felt that after all their support, he owed it to Garth and Chrissie to put them in the picture too.

As he drew up outside their house, he could not see a car outside, but he felt sure Chrissie would be there as he knew she did not go out unless she absolutely had to in an effort to conserve her energy. After seeing her the other afternoon, though, he had to admit that she seemed much better as Garth had said, so he could be wrong, but there was only one way to find out and he parked the car, got out and walked up their drive.

He rang the bell and waited. No reply. He pressed the bell push one more time and to his delight he heard footsteps the other side of the door which was then opened by a smiling Chrissie.

"Ian, what a surprise," she said. "Sorry to take so long. I heard the bell, but I was in the garden putting the washing out. What can I do for you? Garth will be back in a minute, he has just gone to fill up the car for me. Come in."

Ian walked into the house, and followed Chrissie into the lounge.

"I wanted to let you both know what I am up to, but I am sure you can tell Garth when he comes back," he began mysteriously.

"This hasn't got something to do with Pippa, I suppose?" she asked with a knowing look.

"As a matter of fact, it has," he laughed. "We are going up to the Lakes for the weekend and I wanted you both to know that without your support, I might never have plucked up the courage to ask her."

"Oh, Ian, I am so pleased for you and I hope you have a wonderful time. I was wondering in bed last night if I knew Pippa, she must be about my age. Ask her if she ever had ballet lessons with Miss Adams, as I seem to remember there was a Pippa in my class. If so, we could be old friends."

"I will. Wouldn't it be funny if she did remember you?"

Just then the door opened and in came Garth.

"Ah! Entertaining strange men while I am out, are you," he joked, but Chrissie ignoring this comment, said, "There you are at last. Ian has some really good news. I am going to leave him to tell you himself because I must get on, I have several things to do before I collect the twins from school and all mayhem breaks loose. Bye, Ian and, good luck," and with that parting shot Chrissie disappeared off to finish her chores.

"What is going on then?" asked Garth interestedly and Ian explained one more time, what joys the weekend had in store for him.

"Excellent. How did you wangle that one?" Garth asked his friend.

"Obviously my irresistible charm," laughed Ian.

" Perhaps we will finally meet Pippa when you come back. I was beginning to wonder if she really existed," said Garth with a chuckle.

"Definitely, it is a promise," replied Ian, "I also wanted to thank you for taking the time to listen to Tim's CD and for giving him a chance. He is over the moon."

"No problem. I think Nimbus stand a chance in the cut and thrust of the music world. When they have done another recording in our studio, we will know more."

Garth saw him on his way with a pat on the back and a heartfelt, "It couldn't have happened to a nicer bloke."

25

Back home once more, and with his packing done, Ian was sitting in his 'new room' admiring the décor. Without thinking, his hands automatically smoothed down the silky covers of his new cushions and he breathed in the fresh smell of warm, new paint which exuded from the radiators. He was grateful that Mike had persuaded his mother to have a central heating system installed a few years back.

He could hear the faint mumble of a television set through the walls and suddenly remembered his promise to Ivy.

He would have to let her know he was going away for the weekend anyway, so what better time than the present and he could then kill two birds with one stone.

Ivy's home was an eclectic mix of many styles mirroring her taste in clothes. As she sat watching the television, she was wearing a colourful pair of warm woollen trousers in a fetching shade of pink, topped off with a purple sequinned jumper enhanced by some very exotic eastern jewellery.

She and her husband had travelled a great deal, bringing souvenirs back to England with them from every trip. In the hall was a life-size wooden model of a Red Indian Chief wearing a full headdress, whom she referred to as Hiawatha, beside which stood a magnificent brass gong they had found on a trip to Ceylon.

Her sitting room was decorated with heavy flock wallpaper in a warm shade of magenta and there were several brass ornaments from China dotted around the room. Resplendent in the corner, lived an overgrown Swiss Cheese Plant in a big pink and green floral planter, and on top of the old coffee coloured tiled fireplace, sat an ornate china clock with dragons curling round the case, their tongues meeting at the top. It chimed the hours very sweetly, in complete contradiction to the menacing attitude of the dragons themselves.

Ivy was an avid fan of daytime television in the winter. She found the short afternoons and long dark evenings very trying. After all, she could only do so many jigsaws. The different programmes helped her to pass the time.

When her doorbell rang, she was in the middle of a murder mystery and none too pleased at being disturbed. Nevertheless, she got up stiffly out of her armchair and walked slowly to her front door.

"Who is it?" she shouted impatiently.

"It is Ian from next door, Mrs E. I thought you might like that cup of tea I promised you. Can you come round in ten minutes?"

Ivy cheered up immediately, that changed everything. It was Ian.

"I will just turn the telly off Ian. Be with you in a minute," and with that she shuffled off to find her shoes, coat and keys and finally to switch the television off.

Ten minutes later she was walking in through Ian's front door, which he had left open for her.

"Here I am, love," she called as she pushed the door shut behind her. "Where are you Ian?"

Ian appeared at the kitchen door carrying a tray of cups, saucers, a plate of biscuits, the teapot and a small china milk jug, the only survivor of his recent blitz on his mother's china collection.

"Come into the lounge and sit down Mrs E, I'll just put this down on the table."

Ivy followed him into the sitting room, took off her coat and sat down. She surveyed the room critically, then gave her verdict.

"Well done, Ian, it looks very fresh and modern. I like that plant. The only things missing are a few of your Mum's jugs."

Ian laughed. "Sorry, they have all gone now except for this little one," he apologised, indicating the jug from which he was pouring milk into her teacup. "I do have an interesting tale to tell you about one of the others, though," he added with a smile as he poured out her tea. Then he related the tale of the auction and all about the mysterious photograph while she sipped her tea and made the odd appropriate remark. He finished off with, "I almost feel as if Mum was helping me to find Pippa."

"I am not surprised. What a coincidence. I knew Vera always thought that jug was special, and so it proved to be. What a lovely story. I would like to meet Pippa too, she sounds very nice."

"That was another thing I wanted to tell you. We are going away to the Lake District this weekend, so the house will be empty until Sunday night."

Instead of being shocked as he thought she might be, Ivy surprised Ian by saying wisely, "So that is the way the wind blows! I knew something was going on and I am glad. Life is to be lived and it is high time you lived yours, Ian. Drive carefully, won't you and I will see you next week I expect."

With that, Ivy stood up, indicating that their tea party was now over and Ian helped her to put her coat back on.

"I have to get back as 'Countdown' will be on soon and my brain cells need their regular workout," she said, comically tapping her forehead which made her thick white wavy hair bounce up and down. "Thank you so much for the tea. I really enjoyed our little talk, and don't forget what I told you."

What a character, thought Ian affectionately, then he gave her a quick hug and went to see her safely home, leaving his front door slightly ajar.

26

It was getting dark as Ian saw Ivy go inside and shut her door. He turned to walk back up his drive when he noticed some car headlights shining on the road and heard the sound of a diesel engine.

Ian gazed casually towards the lights and realised that it was his brother's 4x4 coming his way. If he intended to visit Ian again, that would be three times in as many days and very unusual. As he waited to see which way Mike was going, the car indicated left and turned into the drive. There was no room for doubt now, he was on his way to see Ian who found himself wondering, somewhat uncharitably, what on earth he wanted this time.

"This has to be a record," he said as Mike jumped down from the car, wearing a very smart blue suit, very shiny black shoes and a rather loud silk tie.

"I am glad you are in, mate," said Mike, ignoring his brother's irony, "because I have been mulling over a plan and I wanted to sound you out before you go away for the weekend. Gaynor told me to leave it until you get back, but I couldn't. I am too up in the air," he started all of a rush. "Shall we go inside?"

Ian was startled and intrigued at the same time and wondered where Mike had been, dressed up like that, but he followed his brother inside the house, saying with a touch of humour, "I don't know if I can take any more excitement Mike, I have just had Ivy Ellison round for a cup of tea."

Mike snorted and disappeared into the house, leaving Ian to trail behind. He found Mike sitting in the lounge waiting impatiently for him to arrive.

"Sit down, Ian. I have just come from the bank where I have been discussing a new project I am contemplating."

He stopped for a moment and looked directly at Ian, who was waiting quietly to see what Mike was going to say next, his eyebrows slightly raised.

"The point is," he began again, "I have an option to buy part of the old airfield with planning permission for several houses and possibly a new school at a later date if the council makes that decision. Anyway, my bit of the development at the moment, will need a new access road, possibly a roundabout and some sewer work. As you know, I can do houses but I have absolutely no expertise in road building. Fortunately, you do. The bank are interested in financing this project, but they know I have no engineers on board and they want me to put a team of professionals together before they will sign on the dotted line. This is where you come in, hopefully. With all your qualifications, you could swing it for me. Are you interested in working with me, Ian? What do you think?" He finished, waiting to see what impact his news would have on his brother.

What a speech. What did Ian think? Actually, he felt as if the air had been sucked out of his lungs. Then he heard Mike's voice again. This time quieter and a bit less confident, it was his turn to feel unsure of himself now.

"I know, you need time to take it all in. I was not expecting a reply today. Think it over while you are away and let me know on Monday."

"It sounds like a good offer," said Ian, having recovered from his initial surprise. "I will think it over. I am flattered you thought of me."

Mike stood up, having done what he came for.

"I know it has come out of the blue for you, Ian, but I have been waiting for an opportunity like this to turn up for some time and I just could not wait to tell you about it and see what your reaction would be. I think it would be good for us to work together and the project is just down your street. I will make sure it is well worth your while, you know. I won't say any more now. If you decide not to do it, there will be no hard feelings." He patted Ian on the shoulder and hurried out to his car. Ian followed him and waited for his brother to drive off before he walked back inside.

Now he understood Mike's unwillingness to chat about his next scheme with him the other day. What a dark horse he was. Ian had no inkling he was cooking up such a big deal, nor had he the faintest idea that he would be included in it. He was also surprised to discover that the idea rather appealed to him and he felt slightly guilty about his initial attitude to Mike's visit as he was offering him a very interesting opportunity. Nevertheless, Ian was now confident enough to know that he was not going to be bulldozed into anything until he was quite sure it was exactly what he wanted.

Of late, his life had resembled a roller coaster ride and he did not know when to expect the next scary ascent or even more hairy descent, whether he could get off the ride, or even if he wanted to. What a good job Pippa would be round soon. She could be his sounding board and he knew any advice she gave him would be sensible and to the point. He had decided over the last few days that it was time he started work again, especially if it was local. He knew one thing for sure; he did not want to leave Pippa for weeks on end, now that he had found her. He decided to send her a text message in the hope that it would hasten her arrival and went looking for his phone.

Pippa was in her kitchen, grabbing a quick salad sandwich when her phone trilled to alert her to an incoming message. She didn't have time for more than that as she was preparing herself for the weekend ahead and had not even done her packing yet. She was planning to do that next, drop off her bag at Ian's, then go home to wash her hair and tidy the flat up a bit before she went to bed. The message was from him and she read it quickly as it was very short.

'Cum sn. Smthng has hapnd. Nd to spk 2 u,' it read.

What on earth could he mean? Well, she concluded, there was only one way to find out . Pippa dragged her bag down from the top of her wardrobe and started to fill it up as fast as possible. It didn't take her long as she had already decided what to take with her and, being intimately acquainted with the vagaries of the Cumbrian weather in winter, the first things to go into her bag were several warm jumpers, her favourite jeans and a waterproof jacket. Pippa eventually zipped up her bag satisfied that she had forgotten nothing and then went down to fetch her car.

She drove round to Ian's house and parked her car behind his on the drive, retrieved her bag from the boot and walked towards the front door. Ian had heard her arrive and was waiting for her with the door open.

"What's up?" she asked him cheerfully, handing him her bag.

"Thanks," he said absent-mindedly, taking her bag and carrying it into the hall. "Mike has just been round and dropped a bombshell on me," he said. "Quite out of the blue, he has offered me a job!"

"And the problem is?" Pippa asked. She was as surprised as Ian, but didn't see it as necessarily a bad thing. "Have you never worked with him before?" she asked, "is that the dilemma?"

"Never and I just didn't see it coming. It is a very tempting offer though, I am glad you got here so soon, I wanted to talk it over with you straight away."

"You are funny, Ian," she said, smiling at him. "When I got your message I thought something disastrous had happened, and you were going to tell me that you had discovered a massive leak in the roof and couldn't go away until it was fixed, or you had broken your arm and couldn't drive. My imagination was running wild."

Ian looked at her ruefully.

"I'm sorry if I worried you, but Mike's offer, coming as it did with no warning, caught me off guard. Anyway, what do you think about it? I feel I am ready to start work again and I have to admit that I quite like the idea of working locally, but working alongside Mike is something else altogether."

Pippa felt sure that once he had got used to the idea, it would not seem nearly so bad as he thought.

"Let's sit down and discuss the whole thing properly," she said sensibly. "We can make a list of the pros and cons if that will help, but first let's have a cup of coffee."

"I would rather have a cup of tea," said Ian laughing.

As he had hoped, she had put things into perspective for him. It wasn't a bad thing at all and if he took up Mike's offer, he would finally have slightly more to offer Pippa with a good job in the pipeline. He followed her into the kitchen and he said gratefully, "I knew you would sort me out!"

Her visit had worked like a charm and, his equilibrium restored, Pippa went home to wash her hair.

Despite the excitement of the previous evening, Ian managed to sleep quite well that night, but at seven thirty on Friday morning he was out for what had now become his ritual run. The weather had settled itself down and there was no hint of rain and only a slight wind to hinder him as he set off.

He was glad Pippa had been round to see him the previous evening. She had brought with her, not only the weekend bag as arranged, but also her calming influence, as he had known she would. It occurred to him as he notched up his second mile, that she was slowly becoming indispensable to him. Mike's new project had been well aired and her advice had been for Ian to sleep on it which he had done and although he had not made a firm decision, he was not so alarmed at the prospect of working with his brother. In fact, he was coming round to the idea that it might just work.

On the way back home, Ian called at the local convenience store for some bottles of water and snacks for the journey, then he jogged the last few yards home. All that was left for him to do now was to have something to eat, take a quick shower and pack the car.

A few hours later, very nearly satisfied that he was ready to go and with the car duly packed, Ian was about to set off to collect Pippa from work, so their weekend could begin at last.

He was looking forward to their trip very much and had bought a map of Cumbria in case they wanted to make a few detours; he had always enjoyed planning journeys and this one was no exception. It had been several months since he had been away from Linchester and it would be good to have a change of scene he thought, especially now with so much to mull over.

He would probably be able to think better away from familiar surroundings and the possibility of another visit from Mike, but best of all, he would have lots of undiluted Pippa time. She did want to go away with him, he had not made the wrong choice; in fact their bond was stronger than ever.

He remembered with satisfaction, that Garth and Chrissie had both been pleased at how things had turned out when he had related the tale to them and when he had explained his plans to Gaynor and Mike, they had been amazingly supportive too. Mike had, uncharacteristically, even given him a big hug and told him he was a very lucky man, but that was old news.

To top it all, Mike had unexpectedly made him that very interesting and potentially lucrative offer of a job.

Ivy Ellison had advised him to live his life and now he felt equipped to do just that, but first there was one last thing he needed to do. He wanted to give Pippa a special gift to celebrate their first trip together and remembered he had seen something in his mother's jewellery box that would fit the bill nicely.

Ian ran up the stairs two at a time and took the box out of the desk in his bedroom. He found what he wanted neatly wrapped in some crisp, white tissue paper and put the little package carefully into his wallet, then he went back downstairs to check everything was switched off and locked up and with one last look around, he walked out of the front door and closed it behind him.

Pippa was waiting for him outside McFarlanes and as soon as he stopped the car, she jumped into the front seat beside him, saying cheerily, "Here I am then."

"Before we set off, I have something to give you, close your eyes," said Ian. Pippa screwed her eyes tight shut and felt him put a small square package into her hand. It weighed next to nothing and she wondered what on earth it could be. "You can look now," he went on.

Eager to see what the surprise was this time, Pippa opened her eyes quickly but all she could see was what appeared to be some carefully folded up tissue paper. She felt the tissue paper with her fingers, then she turned the little parcel over and delved deeper.

The last piece of delicate paper gently parted to reveal a pair of diamond stud earrings in an unusual gold filigree setting, winking seductively up at her. Pippa gasped in amazement and pleasure, but could only manage to breathe one word, "Ian!"

"I guessed that you would like these to celebrate our first trip away. They were Mum's and I wanted to give them from one person I loved very much to another I love even more."

Pippa sighed with pleasure.

"Thank you Ian, they are absolutely lovely," she said, genuinely pleased with his gift and even more overcome by the words that had accompanied its giving. "I am going to wear them straight away."

She removed her beaded drop earrings at once and replaced them with the diamonds, then turned towards him and kissed him with a warmth and tenderness neither of them had ever experienced before.

Ian felt elated. He now knew his old life was finished. He was no longer a cardboard cut-out of a man, somehow, marvellously, miraculously, Ian Chisholm had become himself.

He turned the key in the ignition, indicated right and turned confidently into the traffic as they headed north together.